THE UNTOLD STORY OF MY LOVE

CRYSTAL CATTABRIGA

Dedication

Dad

Prologue

Russell
December 15, 1996

Death is unavoidable for all of us. It is what we do with our time here on earth that matters.

The entire family, including the extended family, emerged from their vehicles to pay respect to my mother, Mary Ann Gonsalves. We gathered around her casket as light rain fell and fog surrounded us. The ones more apt to cry wore sunglasses to hide their tears of sorrow, while others held back the tears, willing themselves to stay strong. I, too, am one of those who held back the tears, and yet the heartbreak consumed my soul for the woman who was no longer here. Many of us stood close together, trying to stay warm as little specks of rain collectively hit our bodies as the priest, Father John, spoke. His voice, filled with compassion, resonated in the air, comforting us in our grief.

I chose not to give a eulogy. I was confident my mother knew the love I had for her without having to list all she had done for me or how she made me feel in front of others. The service at the gravesite lasted about thirty minutes, and when it was over, everyone piled in their cars to my Aunt Bea's house for finger foods and conversation. As I walked away, I couldn't help but turn back, my gaze lingering at the place where my mother's life had ended. This selfless, dedicated, loving mother taught me unconditional love through her actions, and I would be forever grateful.

Many people gathered at my aunt's house, staying for quite a while and sharing memories of my mother and her kindness. I sat quietly, absorbing it all. The tears and laughter from the stories told touched my heart deeply. After the last person left, I kissed my aunt goodbye, expressing my love and appreciation for her opening her home to us all. She hugged me tightly and said, "I loved your mom dearly, and I love you, Russell. If you need anything, don't hesitate to call. Her words of support and love filled me with deep gratitude.

My emotions inhabited me. My heart was heavy with the loss of my mother, but unlike everyone else, I didn't have the luxury of time to grieve. My situation made things a bit difficult as I relocated to Georgia for work years ago and was on a time crunch. Living eleven hundred miles away didn't make things easier. It made the reality of my mother's absence from this world harder to grasp. Being an only child put a significant amount of pressure on me to go through my mother's belongings alone. Sorting through her clothes, jewelry, and personal items reminded me she was no longer here, but I had to do it. Although our connection and understanding of each other was something I cherished, I couldn't help but shake the feeling that she was also sad and sometimes lonely, even if she didn't say it. But I knew one thing to be true about her: she always put me before herself, and I would be forever thankful for that.

As I stepped into my rental car, I embarked on a journey to Solemar in South Dartmouth, my mother's home. I stumbled upon this serene community for her when she turned fifty-five. It was a picturesque haven, nestled away from the city, designed for semi-retired and retired individuals. Despite having a few friends she would occasionally socialize with, she cherished the tranquility and the freedom to live at her own pace. Her love for life's simple pleasures, like solving the crossword in the weekly TV Guide and indulging in Agatha Christie books, brought her happiness.

I arrived just after five in the evening, as the golden light of the setting sun casts a warm, nostalgic glow over the neighborhood. After parking the car and heading to the security door, I noticed Ms. Diaz. The memories of her past conflicts with my mother flooded back. If my mother had an arch-enemy, Ms. Diaz would've been it. She often spoke to my mother impolitely about her grandchildren, Bobby, Crystal, and David, which always led to heated disagreements. Over the years, they both had some choice words for one another, but ultimately, they stayed civil. I watched as Ms. Diaz laid her gardening shears down, heading toward me. She wiped her hands on her half apron as she reached for my hand. I obliged.

"Oh, Russell, I'm sorry for the loss of your mother. I thought the world of her," she conveyed.

Her words threw me for a loop. What, she thought the world of my mother? My response was simple but respectful, reflecting on how I'm taught to respect my elders. "Thank you, Ms. Diaz, for your sympathy and kind words. She felt the same about you."

Yes, I also lied, but there was no point in re-hashing who hurt whose feelings years ago. Also, I heard Ms. Diaz had dementia, so bringing up the past wasn't going to do either one of us any good. As I parted ways with Ms. Dias, I headed for the building. I climbed up the stairs, stood in front of the door, and took a deep breath before pulling out the key from my pocket and opening the door. I stepped in, finding myself looking around. Overwhelming memories hit me like a semi-truck hitting a brick wall. I didn't know where to begin. It felt hard to breathe at times, but all I knew was that I needed to get through this so I could finally grieve in peace.

After several phone calls to family members, I began sorting through her belongings. Piles for donations and items to take back to Georgia started to form. The day quickly turned into night, and I realized I had to leave so I could come back to start again tomorrow. Before returning to the hotel where I was staying, I grabbed something to eat, and as soon as my body hit the bed, I passed out, not waking until seven the following day. Before returning to my mother's, I grabbed a Dunkin Donuts coffee, more boxes, packing tape, and a marker. With an unwavering determination to make progress, I pressed on, refusing to be deterred by the enormity of the task.

By mid-afternoon, all the rooms beside her walk-in closet in her bedroom are packed up. The sun continued to cascade long shadows through the half-open blinds, and the air was filled with the scent of old memories and dust. All my mother's clothes are packed and ready to be donated, which I will drop off tomorrow before flying home. Crouching down, I tossed several pairs of high heels, flats, and shoes from underneath her clothes rack in a box. Checking to ensure I had everything, I noticed a shoe box tucked away in the back. Bending on my knees, I grabbed the box and slid it toward me. Picking it up, a notebook sat upon the shoe box lid—brown twine string wrapped around the entire box, holding the notebook in place with a tag that read: Spring of 1953 in my mother's handwriting.

This discovery, a notebook from the past, carried significant weight. Could these be the letters? The very ones my mother once told me about. The ones that held the essence of their love story. With excitement and trepidation, I untied the string, lifted the lid off with the notebook still cradled on top, and placed it on the floor beside me. Looking in the box, I discovered several envelopes addressed to my mother, Ms. Mary Gonsalves: the return address, Paul Rouleau, my father. Placing the box on the floor, I picked up the notebook. Opening it, the first page, a portal to the past, was titled,

The Untold Story Of My Love.

Written by: Mary Gonsalves.

Finding out that my mother had written a book about her romance with my dad was a revelation that carried a significant, poignant importance. It was not something I could set aside and read later when I returned home to Georgia. Nope, I braced myself for a long night, gathering a few pillows I pulled from the black bag and positioning them against the wall for comfort. Opening the book to the first page, where it all began....

Mary
March 5, 1953

For generations, the belief that everything happens for a reason has persisted. I, too, was a realist, navigating life based on what I believed the outcomes should be. However, the summer of fifty-three marked a profound shift in my perspective. It was a year of complete transformation, altering my life and my fundamental belief about the purpose behind life's events.

My birthplace, New Bedford, Massachusetts, is a city that holds my parents' stories, Joseph Gonsalves and Dominga (Fernandes) Gonsalves Perry. Both immigrants from Brava, Cape Verde, are of Portuguese descent. Their marriage, at the age of twenty-four and nineteen, was a testament to their love and resilience. However, fate had a different plan. My father's untimely death, two months before my birth, left a void. Yet I found peace in the stories my mother shared and the pictures she showed.

From a young age, I was consumed by a deep curiosity about my father. I longed to know everything about him, from his appearance to his character. My mother would share bits of his life to satisfy my curiosity, yet sometimes, I could sense her pain. Now, in my thirties, I realize how difficult it must have been for her to talk about someone she loved and lost so tragically. This understanding has deepened my empathy for her.

My father was a tall, broad-shouldered man with dark, wavy hair. His distinguished appearance often attracted the attention of women, a fact that made my mother uneasy. She found it hard to ignore the disrespect sometimes directed at her, so she often chose to stay home rather than accompany him. From the stories she's shared, it seemed he may not have been as faithful as she had hoped in their marriage, yet she loved him.

She did, however, praise him for his work ethic. He worked full-time as a comber hand, combing sheep wool. It wasn't a glorified job by any means, and he didn't enjoy it at all, but he made a significant sacrifice. He worked every day until he died to provide for my mother and his baby girl, whom he would never get to meet.

Despite the challenges of growing up without a father, my mother, Dominga, always ensured I felt loved. Her role was pivotal in shaping who I am today. She was known as "Minnie" to those who knew her, and she cooked at a restaurant called Rendezvous. As for myself, I was in a job that didn't fulfill me, but unlike my father's situation, I had no kids and was not married, so my options for the future were clear. I'd share my decision to leave with my mother tonight, hoping she would support me.

I'm heading to New York on a one-way ticket to a new life. I've saved up at least six months' wages, hoping to find a better-paying job, preferably in journalism. I'm familiar with city life, so horns blaring from cab drivers, people speed-walking in every direction, and knowing this city never sleeps should be a cakewalk. What won't be a cakewalk is informing my mother that I'm leaving in the morning. She will try to talk me out of it, stating it's too dangerous for a lady like myself to be alone in a big city. I get it, but I will try to reassure her that I am determined and prepared to face the challenges ahead.

Moving out would've been easier if I weren't the last of my siblings left in the house. I have two sisters and one brother, who are both married with children. I want to say I didn't follow suit because I'm too career-driven to care about marriage and kids, but that's not true. I'm just not there yet.

I considered all the questions my mother would ask me, writing several down, assuring myself that I could pass whatever she asked.

1. A place to stay- Check.
2. Interviews for Jobs lined up – Check.
3. Six months' worth of pay saved up - Check.
4. Self-defense against attackers- Check.

As the day of my departure drew near, I could feel the excitement building within me. I had to leave the house by 6:00 a.m., ensuring I did not miss the Greyhound bus at seven. While my mother was at the local meat market, I headed to my room to pack. I was taking just one large suitcase and a small hat box. As I looked in my closet, I packed my Navy blue-white polka dot dress, pale yellow pencil dress, and beloved little black dress.

Each of these dresses symbolized a different aspect of my life. The navy blue dress was for my professional aspirations, the yellow dress was for my optimism, and the black dress was for my independence. I could wear just a simple string of pearls or a colorful scarf with any.

Neatly, I folded three cigarette pants with three different styles of blouses, each with a personal touch that comforted me. The first was a simple button-down light pink blouse; the next was a boat-neck knit blouse, and my favorite was the white ruffle blouse. Knowing I'd need some comfortable footwear, I slid two pairs of ballet flats shoes—one black and the other white—off to the left side, ensuring I still had enough room for my undergarments and toiletries.

As I finished packing, my mother's comforting presence filled the house as she entered the front door. "Mary," she called out. I quickly slid my suitcase and hat box under the bed and yelled, "Be right there." Shutting the bedroom door, I entered the kitchen and found my mother arranging meats in the refrigerator. I smiled and offered my help, knowing she always appreciated it.

She popped her head up, closed the refrigerator door, and asked, "What have you been doing, dear?"

"Just straightening up things in my room," I replied without seeming suspicious.

"Mary, can you please hand me those potatoes behind you on the table?"

Handing them to her, I eagerly offered my assistance in preparing dinner, but she kindly declined, "Honey, I'm good. Thank you for offering, but instead, why don't you pour yourself something to drink and relax in the parlor until dinner is ready."

"Are you sure?" I asked once more.

She brushed my hair back over my left shoulder and encouraged me to relax. That was her way of saying I was in her way, so I respected her space and replied, "Okay, but if you need me, let me know."

"I will, don't worry," she assured me with a warm smile, her eyes reflecting her love for me.

I filled a glass with cold, refreshing water, but not before looking at her. She's been the strongest person I've ever known, yet I could feel the weight of the impending heartbreak I was about to cause. How do I tell her that I'm leaving in just twelve hours? She's been my entire world. Her love for me overwhelms me, and my eyes fill with tears. I turn away, my heart heavy with the burden of my decision. The conflict within me is tearing me apart. I hurried off before she could sense my inner turmoil. I headed into the parlor, placed my drink on the end table, and reached for the book I had left on the coffee table.

I'm immersed in the book **"The End Of The Affair," authored by Graham Greene.** It's the fourth and final book in his series. It has captivated me like no other. The story revolves around Maurice, a writer during World War Two in London, and Sarah, the wife of an impotent civil servant. Despite Sarah's marriage, she and Maurice find themselves in a forbidden love. Maurice's jealousy surfaces when he learns that Sarah is unwilling to divorce her husband, Henry. However, a tragic event that is profound and lasting changes everything.

I'm on the brink of the book's ending, with only six chapters left. The characters' depth and engaging storyline make me torn between conflicting emotions. I was eager to rush through and find out what happened next, but on the other hand, I was reluctant to reach the final page, not ready to bid farewell to the characters I had grown so fond of. Twenty-five minutes into discovering how Maurice's life would change, I heard my mother call my name from the kitchen.

"Mary, dear, dinner is done," she called out.

Tucking my bookmark into page 126, I closed the book and brought it into my room, tossing it on the bed. There was no way I would leave this book behind when I left in the morning. I needed to know how it would all end, and I needed something to read while heading to New York. The thought of the upcoming trip filled me with excitement. The bus ride from where I lived to the hotel where I would stay was five hours. I would be able to finish the book by the time I arrived, hoping the ending would be precisely what I believed it to be.

Walking into the kitchen, my mother pulled a small roast from the oven and placed it on a pot holder before laying it on the kitchen table. It looked delicious. Baby potatoes, carrots, and onions surrounded this juicy piece of meat, waiting for me to eat it. She had warm rolls on a plate with the butter dish on the left and a homemade apple pie on the right. The anticipation of the meal filled the air, and I could hardly wait to dig in. Growing up, I never went hungry from her cooking. Besides missing her, I will miss the meals she prepares.

"Mary, can you please set the table." She asked.

"Of course," I answered, smiling.

As my mother reached for two dinner plates from the China cabinet, she squeezed past me, her love undeniable. She kissed my cheek and whispered, "I hope you know how much I love you." Her words, filled with love and tenderness, warmed my heart.

Either she knew what I was about to tell her, or she was about to say something to me that I didn't know. Whatever it was, I was nervous. I carefully arranged the plates, cutlery, and napkins, ensuring everything was in place, and it was time to eat, but before taking the first bite, we said, Grace. My mother and I were never churchgoers per se, yet we still liked to recognize God for our many blessings. For as long as I can recall, we have always said Grace at the table, a comforting tradition that binds us together.

"Mary, would you like to say Grace tonight?" she asked. Her voice was gentle, and I could feel the weight of her trust in me. It was a moment of connection, a chance to show my respect for our family tradition and express my gratitude for her love and care.

"Certainly, Mother," I responded, eager to fulfill her request and show my respect for what we held dear. ***Dear Father God, in a world where so many are hungry, may we eat this food with humble hearts; in a world where so many are lonely, may we share this meal with joyful hearts. Amen.***

When we were both done scooping food on our plates, my mother didn't take long to start the conversation by asking, "Mary, do you ever think you'll move out, get married, and have some children?"

The question caught me off guard. I slowly pulled the fork from my mouth, swallowing my mashed potatoes, and although they were going down my throat, they didn't seem to be mashed anymore; they were more like lumps. I found it strange that she would ask me such a question. Did she not enjoy my company? Was I disappointing her as a daughter?' I understood my siblings were out of the house and married with children, but I thought we had a good thing going. I thought I must be missing something. My need for validation, for her understanding and acceptance, was becoming more pronounced.

If I'm being honest, I wasn't sure how to answer her question. Did I want to move out? Yes. Did I want to get married and have children? The uncertainty about her question was like a weight on my chest, and I was still trying to figure it out. I knew I wanted a career where I could feel free and discover who I was supposed to be.

I took a sip of my drink before answering. "I'm glad you raised the question of moving out, Mother. I've been wanting to talk to you about my plans. I know this will seem abrupt, but I'm heading to New York tomorrow, and before you say anything, please let me explain," I said, hoping she would give me that opportunity.

"Your support and understanding are crucial to me, and I hope I can count on it, " I conveyed.

Laying down her fork, she took a sip of her drink before she nodded and said, "Please, tell me what your plans are."

I was deeply grateful for her willingness to listen and understand; it meant the world to me, and I hoped she would feel my appreciation and respect for her. Surprisingly, her tone was still the usual loving tone she always used with me. I took a deep breath and said, "Let me start by saying I believe you know how much I love you, and I know you've always wanted the best for me. I have struggled to find my purpose, and no offense, I'm in my thirties, and I still live with you."

"Non-taken," she replied with a smirk.

"I have been working at the same place for years—a factory—where I will never move up in the company or find happiness. I get up every day dreading this part of my life. Yes, I often think about my future. I feel the only way to succeed is to be on my own, get a fresh start, live a little, and yes, maybe after things are going well, fall in love."

Silence filled the air for just a moment. I wait.

"I get it, Mary. I want you to be happy. I never want you to feel like you have to stay for me. Yes, I will be lonely, but getting out into the world and taking risks is something to be proud of. I assume you have a plan for when you get to New York."

"Yes, I do. Let me grab my purse, and I'll read you what I have, okay?"

"Okay." She agrees, her eyes filled with anticipation.

Getting up from the table, I quickly scampered to the bedroom, grabbed my purse from the bed, and returned to the kitchen. My mother could never sit still for too long. I found her cleaning up in the kitchen, so I placed my purse on the chair and helped. Scraping the plates clean, I handed them to her so she could wash them while I put the leftover food in containers placing them in the refrigerator. After drying and putting away the clean dishes, she filled the tea kettle, placed it on the burner, and turned it on.

"I figured I'd make some tea, Mary. Would you like a cup with me? I can slice some apple pie, too, if you like." She offered.

"Yes, Mother. That sounds nice," I answered, trying to calm the butterflies in my stomach that were fluttering from the nervousness and excitement.

The tea kettle began to steam and whistle while my mother cut two pie slices—one for each of us. I took care in preparing the tea, ensuring it was just the way she liked it. Pouring the water into our cups, I added just one spoonful of sugar and a drop of honey, as she had already put the tea bags in. Placing them on the table, I grabbed a napkin setting the spoon on it. As my mother sat blowing on her tea before taking a sip, I retrieved the pocket calendar with everything written down from my purse. In the back of the book were a few blank pages for notes. This is where I had jotted down my plans while in New York. I quickly glanced over it, ensuring I dotted all my I's and crossed my T's.

"All right, I should be good with money, as I've saved up six months' pay, roughly six hundred dollars. I've booked a ticket on a Greyhound bus heading out from the Transit Authority downtown to Boston, where I will climb aboard another bus heading to Midtown, New York. From there, I will stay at Hotel Clinton, on Nineteen West Thirty-first Street. The single room I've rented is affordable until I get a job. In two days, I have a few job interviews, and before you ask, I've taken safety precautions and am prepared to defend myself if necessary. I'm determined to make this work, and I want you to know I have prepared for any challenges ahead. I'm eager to hear your thoughts, Mother."

I waited with anticipation. The look on her face wasn't telling me much. She wasn't frowning or shaking her head. She cut a piece of her pie with the side of her fork before piercing the piece gently, which told me she was thinking. I was sure she was about to eat that piece, but instead, she laid the fork down where it cradled the side of the plate and said, " It seems like you have dotted your I's and crossed your T's. I'm proud of you. The only thing I ask of you is that you please write down the hotel information so I have it. What time must you be out the door to catch the bus?"

"I will be leaving here around six in the morning. My bus leaves the terminal at six forty-five."I replied.

"I'm assuming you've already packed everything you need, Mary? she said, raising her eyebrow as though she already knew the answer to her question.

"Pretty much. I have my toiletries to pack, but I was leaving that for the morning."

We finished our tea and pie while chatting about things I'll experience in New York. I shared places I was excited to see, like the Statue of Liberty, St. Patrick's Cathedral, the Empire State Building, and many more. I could see she was thrilled for me but also concerned as I was going there by myself. I noticed her eyes welled up with tears a few times, yet she did her best not to let one fall onto her face. I reassured her I would call and write to her as often as possible.

The time was well after nine, and we both realized it was getting late, so I helped clean up in the kitchen before heading off to bed, but not before walking over to my mother, holding each of her hands and saying, "Trust me, I'm scared, but a good scare. I need this for myself. There is nothing I want more than to make you proud. Just think, you're not letting me go; you're letting me find my place in the world. I love you with every breath."

At that moment, tears fell down the sides of her soft cheeks. I wiped them away and hugged her tight. My heart felt heavy and burdened, but I knew this was what I needed to do. She looked at me and said, " I know, but I need you to know I will always be here for you, Mary."

With her words echoing in my mind, I felt a sense of peace and purpose. We parted ways, going to bed for the night, knowing our bond was unbreakable and our love would guide us through this journey.

Chapter Two

Seven hours later, I awake to the shrill sound of my alarm clock piercing the early morning silence. Squinting slowly, I opened my eyes just enough to see where the button was to hit snooze for five more minutes. It goes off again shortly, telling me to get out of bed. Pushing the covers off, I reached for my robe, a comforting embrace, wrapping it around myself, feeling the soft fabric against my skin. I slid my slippers on, their warmth and familiarity soothing me, before heading to the bathroom. Looking in the mirror, I noticed the puffiness under my eyes and thought, come on, Mary, don't worry about all that. You got to get moving.

After brushing my teeth and combing my hair, I carefully applied enough foundation, blush, and light pink lipstick to look presentable for going out into the world. Packing up my toiletries, I slipped on my Mary Janes, realizing these would be the only shoes I'd be taking. Somewhere, I would need to make room to put one or two more pairs in my suitcase. Shifting things around, I could only fit one pair, which would have to be my Cutout T-strap flats. I loved those shoes.

Grabbing my suitcases, I heard my mother call out my name, "Mary, are you up, dear? I've called a cab. It's on the way."

I replied, "Yes, mother. Be right there."

Before shutting off my light, I looked around, taking it all in—over thirty years of my life in this small room. It's bittersweet. I flipped the light switch and walked away, knowing I was about to embark on a new adventure. Rounding the corner in the parlor, my mother stood there, her love for me shining in her eyes. I could tell she hadn't slept much, which is understandable. Placing the luggage on the floor beside me, I leaned in to hug her. She held me tight before letting go, a silent testament to her sacrifice and love.

She cradled my face with both hands and kissed me on the forehead. Sweeping a few strands of hair that hung over the left side of my face, she smiled and said, " I don't want to drag this out knowing I'll want you to stay, so I'll tell you, go chase your dreams, Mary. Find your place in this world, and remember that no matter where you are, I'm a phone call away." Her words of encouragement echoed in my mind, inspiring me to step into the unknown confidently.

The cab driver blew his horn, which echoed through the quiet morning streets, letting me know he was outside waiting. Tears began to stream slowly down my mother's face, a poignant reminder of the emotional turmoil she was going through. I wiped them away, feeling the warmth of her tears on my fingertips, reassuring her that I would be okay. With a deep breath, I grabbed my suitcases, feeling my past life in them, and kissed her goodbye one last time before walking out the door to bravely start my new life. The driver was waiting for me with the back passenger door open. He greeted me, "Good morning. Would you like me to put these in the trunk, or would you like to keep them in the back with you?"

" I think they will fit just fine in the back with me," I replied.

He grabbed my suitcases, placing them on the opposite side of the back seat before closing the door. Hoping in the cab, the driver asked, "Where to?"

" Two eighty-four Myrtle St," I answered.

The cab ride was a brief one, just twelve minutes. Glancing at my watch, I noticed that the bus was due to arrive in ten minutes—and the thrill of the impending journey was intense. The real adventure was about to unfold as I eagerly prepared for Boston. As the bus pulled up, I selected a seat near the window, ready to either marvel at the passing cityscape or engage later in a friendly chat with the person who would sit next to me. As the bus gradually filled with passengers, I noticed a gentleman walking down the aisle who looked in his forties descending toward the vacant seat beside me.

He stopped and asked politely, " Is this seat taken, or may I join you?"

He was wearing a gray single-breasted suit, clean-shaven, and had wavy black hair. I didn't get a serial killer vibe from him, but I was still hesitant. Would he be a talker? I hoped he would respect my desire for solitude so I could wake up a bit more. I didn't need a Chatty Cathy this early. Looking up at him, I answered, "No, you can join me."

I stared out the window, minding my business, just waiting for the bus to finish letting people on so we could get going. Once all the passengers were seated, the bus started going. The driver said his morning routine in his receiver, " Good morning. Thank you for riding with Tremblay Bus Company. As we head toward Boston, today's weather will be clear and sunny, with degrees reaching the upper seventies. We will arrive at nine-thirty in Boston, so while you sit back and relax, take in the beautiful scenery or get to know your neighbor."

Morning conversation wasn't necessarily where I shined. I'm a people person, but not at seven. I decided to take the opportunity to read my book, hoping the gentleman would take notice and stay to himself. Reaching into my oversized bag, I pulled it out, opening it to page one hundred forty. Thirty-five minutes later and twenty-five pages into this heart-wrenching novel, the unexpected events catch me off guard, and I'm surprised and emotional.

Sarah finally chooses Maurice but never gets to be with him because she dies. What? Poor Maurice. I couldn't believe I was getting so worked up over it, so much so that the gentleman beside me turned and asked, "Are you okay?"

My face must have turned three shades of red. How embarrassing, I thought. It's probably best to finish the book later. I didn't need this gentleman thinking I was neurotic. My unexpected emotional outburst over the book humiliates me.

"Yes, I'm okay, if you must…"

He cut me off and said, " I'm sorry for abruptly interrupting you. I get it. I have a daughter who loves to read; sometimes, the book gets to her, too. Her words, not mine."

I could see a hint of delight in his eyes as he spoke about his daughter. I took the first step and introduced myself. "I'm Mary, and who might you be?" I asked.

"I'm James. Nice to meet you, Mary."

"Are you going to Boston for business or pleasure?" I asked, trying to make small talk without seeming too nosy.

"I'm going to visit my daughter. She's on spring break from college."

"How wonderful. Your daughter must be happy that you're coming to see her. If you don't mind me asking, what college does she attend?"

"Oh, I don't mind at all. She's at Berkley College of Music, working towards her master's. I couldn't be prouder." He said, his pride evident in his voice.

"Wow. Good for her."

"So, what about you? Are you traveling for business or pleasure?" he asked.

"Actually, both. I'm on my way to New York City. I hope to get a job there and maybe put some roots down to see where life takes me." I shared, sensing a mutual interest in our respective journeys.

"What kind of career path are you interested in?" he inquired, his tone respectful and genuinely interested.

"I love to write, so I'm shooting for something in journalism, but I will be happy just to be a weekly columnist."

He replied, "Really."

His one-word answer puzzled me, but my attention was soon drawn to his briefcase. As he placed it on his lap, I noticed a nameplate near the handle bearing the initials J.P. His fingers deftly slid the three-digit numbers, unlocking the case with a click. He then began to search the side pocket, his actions shrouded in mystery.

As he was about to say something, the bus stopped, and the driver informed us that we had fifteen minutes to get off and stretch before descending to our final destination. We had arrived at the Fall River bus terminal, a bustling hub with people coming and going, their voices blending into a cacophony sound. Some people departed, and others got on the bus. James closed his briefcase, locking it back up, before he turned toward me and asked, "Would you like to get out and stretch? I can go with you if you like."

I replied to his offer, "Yes, that would be fine."

Glancing at my watch, I noted the time: fourteen minutes left. We went to Grace's Coffee and Desserts, just a hundred feet from where the bus parked. James's considerate nature was evident as he held the door for me, letting me enter first. As we joined the line, I noticed three other people were ahead of us, yet time was not on our side.

"Do you think we have enough time? I don't want to be late. You do know that the bus will leave without us, right?" I asked, my concern evident, trying not to seem rude or ungrateful to James's company. I didn't want to get left behind, that's all.

"I believe we will have time," he replied with unwavering confidence. His words soothed my anxious mind.

We had seven minutes, and the line moved swiftly. At that moment, I felt relieved as I heard a woman's voice call out, "Next."

"Go ahead, Mary. Order what you would like. This is on me," James insisted.

The woman who stood behind a worn-out wooden slab counter while the aroma of freshly ground coffee beans filled the air was beautiful and petite. Her hair is swept up like Audrey Hepburn's in the movie One Wild Oat, and coincidentally, she resembles her a little. I chuckled at the thought of Audrey Hepburn working at a tiny hole-in-the-wall coffee shop. As I approached the counter, I ordered a small hot black tea while James ordered a medium coffee with three creams and four sugars.

"Will that be all for you, sir?" the woman asked in a sultry voice as if I were invisible.

I could see she was flirty with James. Don't get me wrong; I wasn't jealous. We were mere strangers, but seriously, did this woman presume I couldn't get a man like James? No class is what she lacked. Her flirtatious behavior made me feel a mix of amusement and annoyance. It was a strange feeling, being entertained by her audacity while irritated by her assumption.

"Yes," James replied, handing her the money and telling her she could keep the change.

When I thought the encounter was over, the woman's actions proved otherwise. She slid a napkin across the counter, revealing her personal contact information and suggesting James could call her for 'Nighttime company.' Her bold and unexpected flirtatious gesture caught me off guard, and I couldn't help but burst into a loud, amused laugh, complete with an unintentional snort, before hastily walking away. James rushed out the door behind me, clearly puzzled. "What? Did I miss something?" he asked.

I turned in his direction and replied, "You didn't find that a bit funny?"

"Not really. I believe the young woman was just being…"

It was my turn to interrupt him. "Let me guess. Was the word you were about to say polite?"

Before he could answer, the bus driver stuck his head out the door and yelled, "Let's go." His untimely interruption only added to the awkward situation, making it even more uncomfortable.

Climbing aboard, the bus driver and I locked eyes, "No beverages are allowed unless it's water, "he declared, his voice carrying a tone of authority that made me feel a bit intimidated.

I rolled my eyes, pondering the day ahead. The worst pick-up I've ever seen just unfolded before me, and now I have to part with my tea. What other surprises does this day hold? Perhaps a pigeon will choose me as its target and crap on me. Or maybe I'll trip and fall, who knows, but whatever the day has in store for me, I'm ready for it. Nothing was ruining this moment.

As I settled into my seat, I checked the time. It was eight thirty, and the bus driver's voice boomed through the speakers, contrasting sharply as he hollered one last time, "Let's go." The sound echoed in the bus. He glanced one final time, looking around for stragglers before sealing the doors. James, who seemed lost in his thoughts, sat quietly, so I turned to the window, leaving him to his musings.

A few moments later, I couldn't help but hear him unlock his briefcase again. I shifted my eyes, trying not to seem so obvious. He reached his right hand and pulled out a small business card. Tucking it inside his suit jacket, he closed his briefcase, then placed it on the floor by his feet. I shifted my eyes back toward the window. The bus was full of people chatting away with each other, yet we sat silently. I somehow felt I might have offended him with my remark about the waitress.

I couldn't take it anymore. I needed to know if I had offended James in any way. Yes, I was the type of person who always needed to make sure I left a good impression on others and cared about other people's feelings. Turning toward him, I blurted out, "Did I do or say something to offend you, James?"

James looked at me, his eyes softening. "No, not at all; I'm just thinking about things." His voice was calm and reassuring. I felt a wave of relief but still asked again.

"Are you sure? You've been quiet since we got back on the bus. Maybe my remarks about the waitress didn't sit well with you. If they didn't, I apologize," I expressed honestly.

"Mary, I'm a grown man who can take a little teasing. You didn't offend me. I was sitting here reflecting on how lucky I have been. Between my business and my daughter, my life is truly blessed. I can't help but feel deeply grateful for all the opportunities that have come my way," James explained.

I said nothing; just a smile of relief spread across my face. Over the next hour, James and I talked about many things. We enjoyed each other's company. As we slowly approached our next destination, the bus driver announced our imminent arrival at the south station. James, reaching into his suit jacket, handed me a small business card. I looked down to read it. The words on the card were a shock to me. I couldn't believe it. I was utterly surprised, my mind struggling to process who he was.

"Mary, you've been so kind to me, and I've enjoyed our bus ride together. As you can see on the card I handed you, I own The New York Herald Tribune. When you have time, call and ask for Dean. He's my VP. Let him know you're interested in the weekly columnist job. Tell him you spoke with me. You still have to interview for the job, but I think you'll be a great asset to the company."

I was stunned, unable to find the words to express my gratitude. I knew I needed to say something, but my mind went blank. With the card clenched in my hand, James grabbed his briefcase, stood up, and said, "May we cross paths again someday, Mary."

The only word I was able to muster up was "Yes."

As I watched James walk off the bus, I imagined the possibility of my dream coming true. This was a once-in-a-lifetime opportunity. As I daydreamed about this new opportunity, the bus driver yelled, " Hello! Miss, did you not hear me? Look around. You're the last one. Let's go; I have a schedule to follow." Despite the bus driver's interruption, my anticipation for the future remained undiminished.

With the business card safely tucked in my purse, I met the gentleman who handed me my suitcases stored under the bus before heading inside the terminal. I checked the time as I felt the anticipation build. There were just a few minutes before they called passengers to board the bus for New York. The excitement of the journey ahead filled me as I made my way to the lady's room. While washing my hands in the sink, I heard a woman's voice announce on the loudspeaker that all passengers leaving for New York should head to the bus as departure is in five minutes.

With a burst of energy, I sprinted across the terminal, my heart pounding. I reached the bus, leaving my suitcases with the gentleman to load and take care of once again. I scanned for a window seat as I stepped onto the bus, but they were all taken. Disappointed, I settled for the second seat from the back. To my surprise, I would share a seat with someone who serves the Lord daily—a nun. Her eyes were closed, and her Bible on her lap piqued my curiosity. As a non-practicing Christian, I found her devotion intriguing. Interesting, I thought to myself. Maybe she's speaking to the big man. Out of respect, I stayed quiet.

Once all the passengers were on the bus, the driver announced, " This bus is heading for New York. If that's not your destination, you've climbed aboard the wrong bus. Now is a good time to get off." His dry humor, delivered with a deadpan expression, elicits a few chuckles. He continued with, "Really? Man, you guys are a tough crowd. Your expected arrival time is twelve-thirty.

We will stop in New Haven, Connecticut, in a little while. This is where you can get out for fifteen minutes to stretch. Until then, sit back and enjoy the open road." His witty banter adds a layer of entertainment to the journey.

Once the driver finished speaking, I pulled out my book, hoping to finish it before we arrived. Although I was disappointed that Sarah never got the happy ending she wanted, I needed to know what Maurice would do now. Turning page after page, I felt broken, yet I felt some gratitude. Sarah's death didn't end without a sense of purpose. Nearing the last few pages, the nun leans over and says, "When you're done reading that, sweetie, I have a bestseller for you to read if you like." My heart skips a beat. Was she talking about her Bible? Her unexpected offer, seemingly out of the blue, caught me off guard.

I wasn't sure how to respond. Did she think I was reading something God would smite me for? The only response I had was a polite smile. She didn't say anything, and neither did I. We just returned to our books—hers being the Bible, and mine a forbidden love affair.

I delved back into the last few chapters and completed the book. The ending was a surprise. Sarah professed to know God, and Bernard eventually found faith in God. It left me wondering how someone's journey could go from forbidden love to embracing God.

After putting my book away, I checked how much time we had left before our next stop. We had an hour left, so I decided, why not talk with the nun? Turning to face her, I said, "Excuse me if I may ask, "How long have you been reading your bestseller?" My voice fills with genuine interest.

She laid her bookmark horizontally underneath a particular verse she was reading and replied, "My sweet child, the Bible isn't a book you read once and then place on a shelf. No, this book is a way of life. I've been reading this book for over forty years."

Raising my eyebrows and shaking my head in amazement, I respond, "Good for you," with a slight smile.

"Yes, this is good for me and can also be good for you. Do you know Jesus?" she asked.

Her question took me by surprise. Jesus? I repeated to myself. I wasn't sure my answer would satisfy her, but I answered her honestly: " I know who He is, but I don't read the Bible or go to church. Don't get me wrong, I have, but I don't think much about it as I probably should."

I could see the expression on her face. She's concerned but doesn't say anything. I wondered if she was secretly praying for my soul or waiting for Jesus to give her a message to tell me.

Either way, I waited. I watched her flip through the Bible, leaving her place in Revelations and flipping to Psalms. Leaning toward her, I tried to see what she was searching for.

" Ah ha," she said as she picked up her Bible from her lap and handed it to me. I held it open as she pointed to the scripture, 32:8: "I will instruct you and show you the way to go; with my eye on you, I will give you counsel."

Handing back the Bible, I pondered why she chose that scripture. I grasped its meaning but was eager for her to unravel its significance. Did Jesus reveal some profound truth about my life that she was aware of but I wasn't? She piqued my curiosity, but before diving into the mystery behind the scripture, she introduced herself, "I'm sister Mary from Saint Patrick Cathedral in New York City, and you are?"

"I'm also Mary, but from New Bedford, Massachusetts."

"That's a beautiful name, don't you think?" she replied, knowing I would agree since it was her name as well.

I nodded in agreement, feeling connected with the stranger who shared my name, and I replied, "Yes. Yes, it is. Can I ask why you picked that scripture for me to read? Did God tell you something?" My tone reflected my sincere curiosity.

Before I answer your question, can I pray over you?"

I entertain the thought and politely reply to her request, "Sure, it can't hurt. Isn't that what God calls people in the church to do?"

"Absolutely," Sister Mary replied.

I wasn't sure if I'd hear her prayer over the loud conversations on the bus, but either way, she was doing God's work, so who was I to stand in her way? She reached for my hand closest to her, laid it in hers, and began praying. Something about this whole situation gave me some sense of peace. It wasn't just that she was a nun, and I believed she had a closer connection to God or that her angelic voice comforted me. It was the sincerity in her words, the genuine concern for my well-being, that she expressed to God on my behalf. That was the first time someone asked to pray for me in a long time.

Before she prayed, I felt anxious and excited, but now it was like a weight had been lifted off of me. My breathing was more relaxed, and I felt a sense of peace.

The bus driver announced we had arrived in New Haven just as Sister Mary finished with, Amen. I offered to accompany her if she wanted to get off the bus to stretch for a few minutes. Her reply made me scratch my head as she asked, "Does Jesus leave the ninety-nine to look for the one, my dear?"

She had me. I had to think about what she was talking about. I was a little rusty on Jesus' parables. Luckily, I understood and said, "Of course he does."

Sister Mary, a woman of faith and humor, laughed as she exited her seat and said, "Mary, I knew you would understand. Her laughter was infectious, and I couldn't help but smile in response, feeling entertained by her light-heartedness.

As we descended from the bus, I pointed across the street toward a sandwich shop, suggesting we could grab something to tide us over if she was hungry. I kindly gave her a heads-up about the rules on the bus, " Here's a little tip, though: whatever you order, you'll have to make sure you either finish it or throw it away. These drivers don't allow anything except water."

"Oh, okay, but you don't need to worry about me. Oh, no, I never waste food, knowing that people go without it every day. I've seen people here and in other countries die because they didn't have food to eat. It's heartbreaking," she replied.

Having ordered a six-inch tuna sandwich on wheat bread and each a bottle of water, Sister Mary and I found a table in the shade to eat. In the quiet of our shared meal, we both seemed to be in awe of God's beautiful creation around us, a feeling that deepened our connection.

Crumpling up my wrapper, I noticed she finished, so I offered to throw her trash away. She handed me hers and asked, " Is it time to get going?"

"Yes. If we don't get going now, we may find ourselves walking," I replied with a slight chuckle.

"Oh no. We don't want that. Do you see what I'm wearing? I wouldn't make it in this heat," She conveyed while pointing to her clothes.

As we safely crossed the street and reclaimed our seats on the bus, I eagerly anticipated the conversation about the scripture she had me read. The bus filled rapidly with familiar faces and a few new ones. A woman struggled to calm her child, but her efforts were in vain. He was shouting and protesting in his seat. Observing his tantrum, I found myself questioning the idea of having children.

The mother's attempts were unsuccessful. Unexpectantly, Sister Mary rose from her seat. Would this be the moment she wielded a ruler? Surely not. I complied with her request, stepping aside in the aisle. She walked three rows up and engaged the child's mother in conversation. Her words are lost to me. The mother nodded. Sister Mary spoke to the child, who appeared frightened before she retrieved something from her pocket, yet I couldn't see what it was.

The child's behavior instantly changed when Sister Mary handed him what she had in her hand. Leaning in, she whispered something in his ear. I watched as a smile spread across his face. He sat back in his seat, captivated by what she had given him. Before Sister Mary returned to her seat, the woman embraced her warmly, expressing her gratitude. It may not have been a miracle, but it felt like one. I never expected the child to stop his tantrum, let alone sit calmly. It was a moment of profound amazement, a testament to the transformative power of Sister Mary's actions.

Sister Mary resumed her seat, and I settled back into mine. The bus driver announced over the speaker that we had an hour left. My mind was buzzing with questions, eager to delve into Sister Mary's life and faith. Why did she choose that particular scripture for me to read? What did she say to the boy, and what did she give him? How long has she been a nun, and did she always feel that it was her calling? The mystery of Sister Mary's life was like a puzzle I couldn't wait to solve.

Just as I was about to question her, she turned to me and asked, "Mary, I haven't had the chance to ask you why you are heading to New York."

I shifted my body from the seat to face her better as I discussed my future goals. I shared my journalistic aspirations yet revealed that I'm unsure of my life's purpose. I don't know why, but I became emotional. A single tear fell on my face. She noticed. Reaching into her left pocket, she pulled a tissue out, dabbing my face; she reassured me it was okay. I felt a wave of comfort, understanding, and connection, overwhelmed by her kindness and wisdom.

"My child, we all go through moments when we wonder about our purpose, but I have good news for you. You're never alone. Psalm 46:5 *reads*, **"God is within her; she will not fail."** You are brave, Mary. Most people don't take risks, and if they do, it's not big ones. If I'm being honest, I've always played it safe. Let me give you an example. After graduating high school, I set my eyes on becoming a nun for two reasons. The first reason is that I needed to escape an abusive father, and the second is I also, like you, needed to know what my purpose was in life," Sister Mary expressed, sharing part of herself with me.

"I'm sorry about your father. I can't image what that must've been like. My father died a few months before I was born, and to be honest, I can't say I miss him, knowing I never had him. So, you became a nun right after high school, then?"

"Not exactly. I first had to accept Jesus into my life and get baptized, followed by many mentorships, courses, and Bible studies. Understanding and decerning God's word in scripture can be tough sometimes, but with a lot of prayer and determination to be close to God, the Holy Spirit helps," She conveyed, smiling.

I was indeed impressed with her dedication to God. She piqued my curiosity about how she knew God existed. Also, why did she read the first scripture to me in Psalms? So I asked, "Sister Mary, why did you have me read that scripture in Psalms? Did the Lord give you a sign?"

Smiling, she replied, "I would like to think it was Spirit lead, my dear. There are times when the Lord uses me to help others. For example, serving at a soup kitchen, passing out Bibles, or even praying for those seeking hope when they attend church. The love of God is everywhere. He is present in this very moment. I don't know everyone's story, but my mission is to share God's love with others. That scripture, I believe, was God letting you know that He has you even if you don't realize it, but you will. Not in your timing, but in His."

I wasn't sure if it was because Sister Mary was a nun or if it was God's presence, but I felt some peace after our conversation. Whatever the answer was, I felt lucky to have met her. As the bus slowed down, I felt a sense of gratitude for the journey and the lessons learned. Peering my head out into the aisle, I noticed we were pulling up at the bus terminal in New York City.

The bus driver announced we were arriving any minute and reminded everyone to take their trash if they had any.

The bus stopped, and the passengers scrambled to collect their belongings. Sister Mary and I waited until most had disembarked before gathering our things. Standing outside the bus, we patiently waited for our suitcases. There, I noticed a small figure tugging at Sister Mary's habit. Stepping closer, I saw that it was the boy from the bus, his innocent eyes filled with curiosity and trust.

Sister Mary bent down to his level. He wrapped his arms around her neck and whispered, "Daddy said he's okay." His words, a comforting reassurance, filled the air with hope. Releasing her, his mother took his hand while they walked away. The boy looked back and waved goodbye.

As the bus driver unloaded each piece of luggage from the side compartment, he called out the names on the tags before placing them on the ground. I waited for Sister Mary to retrieve her bag. I've cherished her company and hoped our paths would cross again. With her left hand, she reached into her pocket and retrieved rosary beads, a symbol of her faith and a source of comfort.

"Mary, God orchestrates our encounters for a purpose, even if we can't fathom it then. I want you to have this. These rosary beads have been a part of my journey since I dedicated my life to the Lord. May they bring you solace, a tangible reminder that God is always with you, guiding you through life's trials. I have a feeling our paths will cross again. May peace be with you," she said, embracing me gently before walking away.

I watched her leave. A sense of uncertainty lingered in the air. Many questions remained unanswered, but the possibility of our paths crossing sometime soon, like a compelling mystery, filled me with hopeful intrigue.

Chapter Three

Hailing a cab, I asked the driver to take me to Nineteen Thirty First St, to the Hotel Clinton. On the ride there, I sat silently, my mind filled with anticipation of being able to rest. The thought of unwinding after being on a bus for several hours was all I could think about. After a 15-minute ride, the driver pulled up in front of a sign that read, "**Unloading Only,**" in big, bold letters. He approached my back passenger side and opened the door for me. Grabbing my luggage from the trunk, he placed it on the curb.

"How much do I owe you, sir?" I asked.

"That will be forty-seven cents, Miss," he replied, holding his hand out.

I handed him two quarters, allowing him to keep the change. I know it was only three pennies, but as my grandmother would say, "Every penny counts." After the cab pulled away, I noticed a tall, distingue, good-looking bellhop standing beside me. He was a vision in his maroon double-breasted jacket with brass buttons down both sides and matching straight-legged pants with a wide belt. His black pill-box-style hat sat upon his head at a slight angle, allowing me still to take notice of his shiny dark, clean-cut hair poking out the sides.

Our eyes locked for what seemed like an eternity. I had never seen someone so handsome in person. He gently brushed my hand while reaching for my suitcases and said, "I can take this for you, Ma'am."

Unlocking my eyes from this beautiful human being while clearing my throat, I interjected and replied, No. Ma'am is my mother. I'm Mary." I couldn't help but chuckle at the situation.

With his left hand on his chest, he smiled and said, "My apologies." His eyes twinkled with amusement, and I could see a hint of a smile on his lips.

As I let go, allowing him to assist me, my left heel caught the curb's edge, causing me to lose my balance. My body tightened, but my arms started flapping like a neurotic bird. Two scenarios were playing in my head as this happened. In the first scenario, I end up in the emergency room with broken bones and amnesia, where the bellhop becomes my male nurse, which is quite fine with me. Yet, in the second scenario, I end up in the emergency room with broken bones, remembering how foolish I looked in front of him.

Either way, I let out a scream, but before I even hit the ground, this man snatched me up with his heroic instinct, cradling my body close to him. I could feel the warmth of his breath beside my neck. Pulling back so we were now face to face, he stood me up and asked, "Are you okay?"

I'm embarrassed, is what I want to say, but instead, I straightened my dress, brushed my hair away from my face, and replied, "Why yes, thanks to you…. I didn't get your name."

"It's Paul," he answered.

Extending his hand, I extended mine to be courteous, knowing he just saved my life. Bringing my hand to his lips, he kissed it and said, " I've never swept a woman off her feet. I guess there's a first time for everything."

Quickly pulling my hand from his, I politely replied, " Sir…"

He interjected with a sarcastic remark."Sir, is my father. I'm Paul."

What? I didn't have time for whatever this was. Did he think I allowed men to kiss me whenever? Did he think I owed him for saving my life? Whatever he thought this was, it wasn't. Asserting my independence, I calmly said, " If you just take my suitcases and place them in the lobby at the desk, I can take them to my room myself."

"Mary, did I offend you? he asked.

"Please, Paul. I can do it myself."

"It seems I've upset you. I deeply apologize. Please, let me take them to your room. It is my job."

Ignoring his plea, I opened my purse and tipped him before entering the lobby. As I approached the front desk, I noticed a well-dressed gentleman handing a room key to a couple.I waited for him to finish before announcing my arrival, but he beat me to it with a warm greeting. "Welcome to Clinton Hotel, Ma'am." He had an Italian accent.

I smiled politely, noticing his name tag pinned to his black-and-white tuxedo. I replied, "Thank you, Sergio."

I used his first name out of respect, as my mother taught me it's polite to address people by name when possible. She said it's more personable. With Paul behind me, I stepped to my left, focusing on Sergio. I didn't turn toward Paul, but I did acknowledge his presence. I pulled out my ID from my purse. I told Sergio that I'd be staying at the hotel for several months and had called ahead.

"Ah, Ms. Gonsalves, I see right here that you will join us for some time and stay in room three hundred and seven. If you can sign below on this line, I can give you your key," he requested.

While reading over and signing the room agreement, Sergio told Paul, "Please take Ms. Gonsalves' suitcases and show her to her room." Before I could tell Sergio I was more than capable, Paul picked them up, ready and willing to do what his boss required. The service and Paul's sincere smile made me feel genuinely cared for, yet I was still irritated with him, a feeling I struggled to suppress. Placing the pen on the counter, Sergio put the agreement in a drawer to his right and handed me my room key.

"If there is anything you need or I can do to make your stay more pleasurable, please don't hesitate to call or come by the desk. Let me reassure you that our hotel takes the safety and security of our guests very seriously. We have twenty-four-hour security personnel, so you have peace of mind while you stay with us. Once again, thank you for choosing Hotel Clinton, Ms. Gonsalves." Sergio genuinely expressed, making me feel secure and well taken care of.

"Thank you, Sergio, you're very kind."

As I followed Paul towards the elevator, I was struck by the grandeur of the hotel's interior. The sight was truly awe-inspiring. The lobby was adorned with numerous Crystal Chandeliers that hung from the ceiling, casting a warm and inviting glow. To the right was a cozy lounge where guests engaged in casual conversation, smoking, and sipping drinks. Three large white pillars reached the ceiling several feet from the lobby, adding a sense of grandeur. The opulent ambiance of the hotel's interior was genuinely inviting. The elevator chimed one soft ding, and the doors opened, inviting me to explore further.

As I stepped aside to let the woman on the elevator enter the lobby, several men followed her closely. As she passed me, I couldn't help but do a double-take. Was that Marilyn Monroe who walked past me with such grace and elegance? I wondered. Stepping into the elevator, I turned back to face the lobby, my eyes still fixed on trying to figure out who she was.

Paul noticed my expression and said, "Yes, Mary, you saw correctly. That was Marilyn Monroe. She's staying here at our hotel. I'm told one of her movies, Gentleman Prefer Blondes, is being shown at the Tri-City Drive-In. There's a press release happening somewhere tonight."

The unexpected encounter with a Hollywood legend, Marilyn Monroe, added a significant touch of intrigue to my hotel experience, leaving me pleasantly surprised. The elevator doors closed as Paul pushed the button for the third floor. Seconds later, we arrived, stepping out; I followed him down the hallway.

Standing in front of room three hundred and seven, I pulled out the key and opened the door. Paul followed me in with my suitcases. "Where would you like me to put these down, Mary?" he asked.

I pointed toward the bed and said, "Beside the bureau will be fine, thank you."

He did what I asked and apologized again before heading for the door. I watched as he left, wondering if I should've stopped him, but I didn't. I might have taken his gesture of kissing my hand too far, but I didn't want him to think I was some two-bit hussy who allowed strange men to kiss me whenever they wanted. Maybe this was how men treated women in New York, but that wouldn't happen back home.

My stomach started to rumble, and I was getting a little hungry, so I checked my watch to see what time it was. Lunchtime was over, yet it was too early for dinner. To kill a little time, I decided to unpack. The room was small but manageable. A twin bed, invitingly comfortable, was against the left wall of the room, a bureau across from it, and a small, seven-inch black and white TV sat upon a small stand in the corner close by the window that overlooked the side street. It didn't take long to get all my stuff situated, so I decided to rest for a while, but not before calling the front desk for a wake-up call. Sergio answered the phone.

"Good afternoon, Ms. Gonsalves. How may I be of service to you?"

"Sergio, If you could be so kind, ring my room in an hour. I'm going to take a quick nap."

"Yes, Ms. Gonsalves. Is there anything else I can do for you?"

"No. That will be all. Thank you."

Sliding off my shoes, I pushed them to the side of the bed and lay down, trying to get comfortable. I tossed and turned for a little bit before dozing off, but it didn't take long for me to be awake again. Loud sounds from a garbage truck outside my window awaken me. There was no way I was going back to sleep anytime soon, so I decided to freshen up and prepare to head out. I ensured I had my room key before locking up and going to the elevator. The doors opened, and I stepped in, but before I could push the button for the lobby, it closed on its own and started moving.

As the doors opened, I stepped aside, expecting to see a stranger. To my surprise, it was Paul. He stepped in, nodding in acknowledgment. Of all the people, he would be the one to get on my elevator. This unexpected encounter added a twist to my day. It should have been a quick ride, considering we only had two floors before reaching the lobby, but luck was not on my side.

The doors opened on the second floor, and a young couple stepped in behind me. Seconds later, I heard them giggling, and it sounded like a make-out session behind me. Neither had self-control with their hands and lips long enough for a five-second ride to the lobby. Talk about uncomfortable situations—well, for me, anyway. They seemed comfortable. I kept my face forward, minding my own business. Between the heavy breathing and lip-smacking, I was sure one of them would've passed out. Glancing in Paul's direction, I noticed he was grinning from ear to ear. What kind of man enjoys this perverted elevator ride, I thought?

I stepped out when the elevator halted, and the doors slid open. The young man winked in my direction as he walked past, holding his lady's hand. Never in my life, I thought. Suddenly, I heard a voice over my shoulder remark, "To be young and in love."

Turning sharply toward Paul, I retorted, "I'm not a prude, but there's a time and place for public displays and affection. A lady would never, and I certainly wouldn't."

"Mary, not everyone is a lady, nor a lady like you," Paul remarked as he stepped toward the lobby door and exited the building.

Whatever I thought, my beliefs were unwavering. Walking up toward the counter, Sergio said, "Ms. Gonsalves, I was just about to ring your room. Is everything all right?"

Laying my purse down, I answered, "Yes, Sergio, everything is fine. Is there a phone I can use?"

Pointing to a single phone booth across the lobby, he inquired, "Do you need some change, Ms. Gonsalves."

"I have some, Sergio, thank you."

Grabbing my purse, I walked over to the phone. Dialing, I waited as the phone rang several times before my mother answered, " Hello."

"Hi, Mother. It's Mary."

"Mary, It's so good to hear your voice. Are you in New York? Are you doing well? What's it like out there? Are you safe?"

She bombarded me with so many questions that all I could do was laugh and answer, "Ma, I'm good. Yes, I'm in New York."

"Have you met anyone yet?" She inquired.

"Have I met anyone during my time here? I just arrived a couple of hours ago," I reminded her.

" I know. I just wasn't sure if you met any friendly city people yet. You know you have to get out there. Introduce yourself to people. Don't be a hermit. Socialize."

"Mother, I've been here for less than two hours. In time, I'm sure I'll meet people."

"Okay, Mary. I'm sorry. I'm just excited for you. Maybe you'll meet a nice man while you're out there. It wouldn't be so terrible for you to fall in love. Maybe get married and have some children. I'm just saying."

"Yes, I get what you're saying. Let me figure out things before you push me into finding a man and having kids, okay?"

"Alight," she said, sounding a little disappointed in my decision for love.

"I'm going to hang up now. I'm about to grab a bite before returning to the hotel for the day. I love you, and I'll call you on Sunday."

" Okay, Mary. I love you. Please be safe, and don't forget to call."

After hanging up, I shook my head, thinking I'd be questioned like this every time I called her. I know it. Making my way outside the hotel, I pondered my next move. There, I noticed a man standing nearby, smoking a cigar. I decided to take the initiative and approach him. "Excuse me, sir, could you recommend a good place to eat? Not too far, if possible?"

Blowing smoke in my direction, he answered with a gruff, deep smoker's voice, "About six blocks, there is a place called Crossroads Café."

Waving my hand to clear the smoke traveling toward my face, I asked, " Is there a place closer than six blocks?"

"Lady, do I look like an information booth? I told you where you could eat," he said as he put his cigar out on the side of the brick building before tossing it on the ground and walking away. I brushed off his short-tempered rudeness, keeping an open mind about the people here. I hoped not all people here were like him. Maybe he was having a bad day.

It was just before five, and the streets were still busy with people trying to get somewhere quickly. My mother always said you could never be too safe, so I put my purse strap over my head across my body. Quickly pivoting around to head down the street, I noticed Paul talking to a thin, young blonde woman standing just a few feet from me. She's laughing while touching his jacket. I didn't want him to see me looking, but he caught me.

Despite jealousy and my burning curiosity, I swiftly brushed it off. I couldn't fathom what had come over me. Why would I have a jealous feeling? I just met him. Turning my back toward him,I began walking in the opposite direction. It was then I heard him call out my name. I pretended not to hear and continued my journey. Suddenly, a hand touched my shoulder. I spun around, ready to call for help, only to find it was Paul. I felt like I couldn't catch a break with this guy.

"Hi, Mary. You okay? You look lost?"

"Yes, I'm fine. Is there something I can help you with?" I asked, trying not to be annoyed, but the irritation was evident in my voice.

"No. I'm sorry I bothered you," he answered, walking away as he shook his head.

Despite the distractions, I was determined to stay focused. I pushed Paul out of my mind and continued walking down several blocks before coming to a crosswalk. While waiting, I observed several people press the button on the pole, hoping it would change faster. I wondered how many times a day people did that, knowing it wouldn't make a difference. The light changed, letting the cars know to stop, and everyone proceeded in a fast herd-like motion, swiftly crossing the street, including me. Looking to my right, I spotted a long horizontal building with a sign that read, Crossroads Café'.

My stomach grumbled, and I couldn't wait to get off my feet and eat something. Making my way to the front door, I passed several sidewalk vendors selling all types of goods. One man had many suspenders over his right arm while he yelled, " Good quality suspenders for only nine dollars." At the same time, another man opposite him was selling shoestrings for ten cents a pair. Weaving in and out of people, I entered the café'. There was a sign that read: Seat yourself.

I looked around to find a small table near the front window. This way, I could people-watch while I ate. Shifting my eyes, I noticed a young woman and her daughter waving in my direction.I thought there must be someone standing behind me. I glanced over my left shoulder and then over my right, but there was no one.

The daughter, a picture of innocence at around ten, rose from her seat and approached me. She wore a pale yellow dress, and her feet were adorned with white Mary Jane shoes. Her sunshine blonde hair was neatly pulled back in a ponytail. With a warm smile, she halted before me and said, "My mom would like to know if you want to join us."

I was confused as I didn't know either of them. Peering over at her mother again, she waved me over. Looking down at this little girl, I replied, "I think your mother has me confused with someone else, sweety. I don't know your mom."

She giggled with anticipation and answered, "I know. We saw you in the hotel where we are also staying. She told me to come get you so we can eat together." Grabbing my hand, she said, "Come on. I'm hungry."

I followed her to the table by the window overlooking a busy street. The woman stood. She wore a red and white polka dot swing dress with a beautiful matching white pearl necklace and earrings. Part of her wavy brown hair is pinned on the left side with a big white flower clip, while the right side is swept up with a curl pinned away from her face. She placed her left hand on my back, pointed to the chair her daughter pulled out, and said, "Sit. Join us. I'm Sylvia, and this is my daughter Ruth."

They seem like kind people, so I obliged. I introduced myself: "I'm Mary. It's nice to meet you, Sylvia and Ruth."

When the waitress came over, Sylvia, with her reassuring smile, said that she had been here several times and recommended the cheese pizza or turkey club sandwich with fries, depending on how hungry I was. Not worrying about looking at the menu, I trusted her and ordered the turkey club with fries and a Coca-Cola. She and Ruth decided to split a cheese pizza, both drinking rootbeers. As we waited, Sylvia and I got to know each other while Ruth colored on a piece of paper her mother pulled out of her purse.

"So, Mary, what brings you to the Hotel Clinton? Business or pleasure?" she asked, smiling.

"I'm here for a job?" I replied.

"Interesting. Do you live somewhere in New York, or did you move from somewhere else?"

"I moved from Massachusetts. The job I worked for some years paid okay, but I didn't see myself there long-term. I felt like I needed a change."

" Good for you. Being brave and all. I don't want to presume, but I noticed you were alone when you arrived at the hotel. So you're single?"

"Yes, happily. I mean, someday, maybe, but right now, I'm trying to focus on my career."

"Honey, I get it. I married young. My husband is a good provider, a good man, but a terrible husband," she whispered in the last part, not letting her daughter hear.

While we enjoyed one another's company, Sylvia confided in me about her marriage. She told me that she and her husband have an agreement. As long as Sylvia cared for Ruth, she could go anywhere, do anything, and buy anything. That would satisfy some people, but Sylvia would trade it all for her husband's attention. It was clear that she loved him deeply.

He travels for work and has them come along so he doesn't feel alone. Sylvia said he tries to be attentive in their marriage but still wishes it was more. Throughout our entire time at the café, Ruth behaved very well, which was impressive, given her age. I noticed the time and told her it had been a long day for me and that I needed to rest. Before parting ways, we planned to meet again Saturday morning for breakfast and then walk in the city.

Arriving at the hotel, I passed the front desk, where Sergio asked if I needed anything. I assured him I was all set, and if I did, I'd call. I couldn't wait to take off my shoes and relax in the bathtub before crawling into the bed. The thought of the warm water and soothing bubbles already brought a profound sense of relief. The elevator made it up to my floor without stopping, for which I was grateful. No Paul nor a make-out session was going on behind me this time. Searching in my purse for the key, I heard a woman call my name. I turned around. It was the housemaid with her hand stretched out and an envelope in it.

"Ms. Gonsalves, I was asked to give this to you, " she expressed.

"Who's this from?" I asked.

She shrugged and replied, " I do not know. I do not clean his room. He just passed me by in the hallway and asked me to give this to you."

It was peculiar that the housemaid didn't know the sender, but I accepted the envelope nonetheless. As she walked away, I unlocked my room and tossed my purse on the bed, eyeing the envelope. It bore only my first name, no last name. I initially thought it might be from the hotel, but they would have included my last name. This sparked my curiosity. I tore it open. Instead of a letter, I found a small handwritten note. It read:

Mary,
I'm writing to you hoping you will forgive me.
I did not mean to offend you or make you uncomfortable. Please accept my apology.
Sincerely, Paul.

My heart ached at the thought of this man feeling so distressed that he felt he needed to pen an apology. That was never my intention. I was determined to seek him out tomorrow, hoping to mend our rift, but for now, it was late, and I needed to prepare for bed. I placed my watch on the bureau before heading into the bathroom to run a soothing bath. As I undressed, I stepped in, letting the warm water surround me, easing the day's tension. I stayed in the bathtub until it lost its warmth.

After drying off and getting dressed, I walked toward the window, closing the drapes. Turning on the TV, I searched for something to watch. There wasn't much of a selection, as only four channels existed. I stopped when the gentleman said, "Coming up, next, I Love Lucy show." I never really watched that much television, but whenever I got the chance to watch Lucy and Desi, I made a point to watch it. Pulling down the cover, I climbed into bed and got comfortable.

Thirty minutes later, I rolled over and went to sleep when the episode ended. I didn't bother shutting off the TV, hoping it would drown out some city noise.

Chapter Four

I tossed and turned most of the night, waking to a horn blaring outside my room. Looking out toward the window where the curtains didn't close completely, I could see a glimpse of the sun. Getting dressed, I applied a slight rose color blush to my cheekbones and a soft pale pink lipstick to my lips before I headed out. Locking the door, I made my way toward the elevator. Once in the lobby, I pulled out John's business card and called, asking for Dean at The New York Herald Tribune. The receptionist on the phone put me on a brief hold after asking what the call pertained to.

A deep voice answered, "Hello, this is Dean. How may I help you?"

"Good morning. My name is Mary Gonsalves. I'm inquiring about a position you may have available."

"Who did you say you are?" he asked, slightly annoyed.

"Mary Gonsalves, sir. I met your…."

He cut me off mid-sentence, "Unless you have an appointment or put in an application, you are wasting my time and yours."

"Sir, I apologize. I didn't mean to upset you; it's just that I was told to call and ask specifically for you."

"That's what they all say. This won't get you the job any faster. I have back-to-back meetings all day and don't have time to be on the phone. My advice is to make an appointment next time," he stated as he hung up.

Despite the discouraging conversation, I was not ready to give up. I was determined to secure an interview and get the job. I had come to New York for a fresh start, and I wouldn't let anyone stand in my way. As I put the card back in my purse, I reassured myself that today would be a good day, so I decided to march on over to talk to Dean in person. Sergio greeted me as I walked past the counter toward the hotel doors.

"Good morning, Ms. Gonsalves."

"Please, call me Mary, " I replied, stopping for a quick chat.

He smiled and asked, "How was your first day in New York?"

"It was lovely. I didn't do or see much. Before turning in for the night, I did grab something to eat and met Sylvia and Ruth. They were very kind."

"Yes, they are one of our top guests here at the hotel. Beautiful family. Well, I'm glad you've had a pleasant time, even if it's been one day. Remember, if there is anything I can do for you while you are staying with us, please don't hesitate to ask."

"Thank you for your kindness, Sergio. Have a wonderful day."

Stepping out of the hotel, I noticed Paul loading suitcases onto a gold rolling cart as a couple paid their cab fare. The sounds of the city traffic filled the air, and the warm New York sun cast a glow on the pavement. We made eye contact. He smiled sheepishly as he waved in my direction. Walking toward him, I leaned over his right shoulder and said, "I don't want to bother you while you're working, but I was just wondering what time you get off today?"

"I clock out at four 'clock," he replied.

"Can we meet up in the lobby at that time?" I asked, my heart beating faster, anticipating his reply, hanging in the air like a delicate thread.

His silence was deafening, and I couldn't help but feel disappointed. Before he could answer, the couple told him to get moving with their suitcases as they followed behind into the hotel. I could wait, hoping he returned in a few minutes, but I felt like my window of opportunity for this job was ticking. Uncertainty gnawed at me, and I didn't want to take a chance, so I left.

Several blocks later, I arrived, standing in front of what could be my big break. I told myself to pull it together, take a deep breath, and confidently walk in as if the job was mine. I was about to open the door when a gentleman in what seemed to be a costly suit blew by me. Turning around, I watched the driver open the door as the gentleman climbed in. I couldn't help but wonder if that was Dean.

The thought of a missed encounter with Dean filled me with disappointment. Part of me wanted to tap on the back passenger window, getting his attention, but I'd probably come off crazy, so I didn't. Instead, I watched as the car drove off. Quickly heading inside, I asked the woman sitting behind the shiny silver desk if Dean was available. She informed me that I had just missed him and that he would be back around four o'clock.

Of course. That was just my luck. If I leave to try and meet up with Paul, I might lose the opportunity to get this job, but if I stay waiting on Dean, I'll miss Paul. I decided to wait on Dean. After all, I was here to better my career, not start a romance with a stranger. Looking at my watch, I realized I had half the day to kill. Luckily, it was a beautiful day, and the temperature was just right for walking in the city.

I strolled down several blocks, stopping at the New York Public Library. The architecture was a sight to behold—it was stunning—the hanging lights, shiny floors, and exuberant books. I filled out a library card to search for my next great novel to read. I'm a sucker for sweet romance and a good mystery. Walking up and down the aisles, I'm overwhelmed by such great authors. Which one, or ones, shall I read? I saw a few Agatha Christie books on the shelf, which piqued my curiosity. After reading the synopsis, I chose **The Mysteries Affair at Styles**. I felt this would be a good one. I looked around a bit more before checking the book out.

Finding a small grassy area outside the library, I sat under a tree to read a little of the book to pass the time. The city streets were filled with people continually passing by. Some were heading somewhere important, and others, like myself, were trying to fill their day with something to do. My concentration from reading was broken when a woman sitting nearby pulled out a sandwich and began to chew with her mouth open. It was disgusting, yet it made me hungry. I know that didn't sound comforting, yet true.

The woman caught me staring at her and asked, "Would you like half?" as she stretched out her hand.

Embarrassed, I smiled and replied, "Oh no. I'm okay. Thank you, though."

Bringing her hand back, she took another bite and chewed with her mouth open again. I couldn't take it, so I dog-eared the page of my book, got up from the grass, brushed myself off, and headed on my way. Strolling a few blocks up the street, I stood before St. Patrick's

Cathedral. The architecture was breathtaking, but I became distracted by a delicious aroma wafting in my direction. It was then that I spotted a food truck across the street. My stomach started to growl like a pack of wolves. I couldn't take it.

I walked across the street with such confidence in my decision. It was there that the man and I made eye contact. "What will it be, young lady," he asked, ready to serve me.

"I'll have one of those giant cheesy slices of pizza and a bottle of water, sir," I answered, as my mouth was already watering at the thought of the grease and cheese sliding down my stomach.

Tossing it on a paper plate, he handed me the slice, a few napkins, and the water. "That will be twenty cents, please," he said.

After paying the man, I spotted a bench against a clothing store building. I strolled over to sit where I could devour this cheesy goodness of dough and sauce. My taste buds tingled with happiness as the rumble in my stomach subsided. Rinsing it down with cold water hit the spot. When I was done, I looked for a trash can but couldn't find one, so I crumpled up the paper plate and napkin, tucking it in my purse. Walking back toward the church, I couldn't help but notice all the intricate details around me, from the buildings' architecture to the flowers' colors.

Stepping inside St. Patrick's Cathedral, there must've been a hundred people walking around. Many admired the statues and Biblical quotes, while others sat in the pews, taking in the presence of God. I walked up toward the front, where, at the end of the pew, a young Portuguese lady was weeping softly as she wiped tears from her face. I didn't know what to do, but my heart ached for her. I sat near her in silence. Turning in my direction, she said, "Isn't He good? Yet, we don't deserve His mercy and grace."

Her emotional state was profound, and in that moment, we shared a deep connection of empathy. I wasn't sure if she wanted me to answer or if it was a rhetorical question, so I politely smiled. She opened her purse and pulled out a small, pink, compact mirror with a rose shape on the cover. Checking her face from her fallen tears, she turned in my direction and asked, "How do I look?"

"Honestly, you look fine. I don't even think you messed up your make-up. If it were me, I would've been a hot mess," I stated, trying to give her ease. She was wearing a simple yet elegant dress, her hair neatly done, with a hint of nervousness in her eyes.

"You're too kind, sweet friend. What is your name?" she asked with a tone that resonated with genuine respect.

"I'm Mary, and you are?"

As she put her compact mirror back in her purse, she reached out her hand and said, "I'm Isabella, from Harlem. It's so very nice to meet you, Mary, from?"

"Oh, sorry. I'm from New Bedford, Massachusetts. I just moved to New York hoping to get a better job."

"Did you come to the church yourself, or are you with someone?" she asked, her curiously piqued.

"I came here alone. I've only been in the city for a day. I arrived yesterday in the afternoon."

"Oh, I see. I'm also alone. I can only imagine how it must feel to be in a new city and not know anyone. If you would like, I was going to walk through Central Park. Would you like to join me?"

I checked my watch. I had three hours to kill before I needed to be back if I was going to meet Dean. That should be enough time, I thought. "Sure, as long as I'm back here in this area before four," I expressed.

"Of course. Let me pray for my filho, and then we can go."

She bent down on the kneeler and prayed while holding her rosary beads. I stepped away to give her privacy. This sweet lady, seemingly around my age, was praying for her son. I wondered what was wrong with him. Maybe nothing; maybe she just always came here to pray for him. I didn't want to ask or speculate. We left the church when she finished praying, but not before she stopped at the Holy Water stoup. Dipping the tip of her pointer finger into it, she touched her forehead and kissed the side of her hand.

The walk took us roughly fifteen minutes. When we arrived, we found a bench in the shade where we sat chatting with one another. She asked many questions, and I answered them all. I felt as if we had known each other for years. It wasn't until I started asking her about her life that she didn't reply with much. Most were one-word answers. I couldn't help but feel a little disappointed, as I was eager to learn more about her, but I understood. We were strangers. I was just grateful for her company.

Then, she said, " Forgive me, for my life isn't that exciting. I've always wanted to leave New York and travel the world, but I could never leave my parents. As a small child, I dreamt of being a well-known photographer whose photos would be in The National Geographic magazine. Unfortunately, I had to put that dream on the back burner due to my mother getting ill three years ago from Cancer.

My dad owned a bodega for many years until he had to sell it to pay my mother's medical bills. In the end, it didn't save her. We lost her last year, and then, from all the stress of it, my dad suffered a heart attack six months later and died. But through it all, my faith in the Lord and our family has remained unbreakable, a source of comfort and support. I have one brother who was living in the Bronx doing construction, but when my parents both died, he sold his place and moved back to Harlem to be with me and my son."

It might sound unusual to many, but Isabella's resilience is truly inspiring. Despite losing both parents within a year and yet she continued to push through. Her strength is a testament to the human spirit's ability to overcome even the most challenging circumstances. Finding the right words is often difficult in the face of such tragedy. All I could do to express my sorrow was hold her hand. She smiled. We sat silently, enjoying the warm summer breeze that passed us by occasionally. Curiosity stirred inside me about her son, but I did not want to push her, as she had already shared personal things with me.

As she took a sip of the water she had pulled out of her bag, she asked, " So, you're not married and have no children; what's that like?"

"It's okay, I guess. Maybe someday, but I can't imagine trying to make time for a husband and children. I would fail miserably, " I confessed. That's when she opened up about her son.

"You know, I have a seven-year-old son named Mateo who's in second grade. This kid is brilliant. Smart as a whip. He loved playing outside, especially soccer. He could've been the next Alfredo Di Stefano if God wanted him to be."

I couldn't take it anymore. I had to know, so I humbly asked, "You said he used to play outside; what's wrong with him, Isabella?"

Tears began to stream down her face. I hurried to open my purse, pulled out tissues, and said while handing them to her, "I'm sorry. I should've minded my business."

Taking a few deep breaths, Isabella slowly stopped crying as she wiped her face dry. Balling the tissue in her hand, she said, in a soft, fragile tone," Mary. It's been tough for me this week. You caught me on a bad day. I feel like a basket case." Her vulnerability was intense, but her strength was even more so.

"No, Isabella, there's no reason to apologize. I should've minded my own business," I conveyed, feeling a mix of guilt for prying and empathy for Isabella's situation.

Laying the tissues on her lap, she reached into her purse and pulled out a photo. She held it in her hand momentarily before handing it to me. With tears in her eyes, she began to tell me his story, "This little boy, this is my Mateo. He is my world, my heart walking outside my body. A couple of months ago, Mateo started getting fevers, headaches, and throwing up. His doctor said he needed to be sent to Boston Children's Hospital for some tests. It was there that several doctors confirmed Mateo contracted polio.

As of right now, there is no cure. My Mateo resides at the hospital on an Iron Lung machine. It is a negative pressure ventilator. It assists breathing when muscle control is lost. I haven't been able to hold or tell him everything will be okay. His condition is severe, and the doctors have told me that his recovery if he recovers, will be a long and challenging journey."

Her voice resonated with love as she spoke about him, her faith unwavering, even in the face of the unknown. I couldn't fathom the heartbreak she was enduring, but I could sense her belief that God would guide her son. As I gazed at Mateo in the picture, I examined his face, thinking, what a precious boy. I handed her the photo back and said, "Your steadfast faith for Mateo is inspiring. He is such a handsome little boy."

As she tucked the photo back in her purse, her words touched my soul when she replied, "Thank you for your kind words, Mary. Do you know why I was at the church today?"

It was apparent, but I answered, " You were there praying for Mateo."

Staring up at the sky filled with bluish-white clouds as the warm air floated by us, she said, "Yes, that's right. As tired as I am every day after work, I catch the train to the church, where I sit in the same spot and pray to God. My heart is filled with sadness and worry, yet my faith is not shaken. I know God isn't doing this to my boy, yet I'm human, and sometimes I get angry at God, but that doesn't mean I don't love God. I know Mateo's chances are slim, but he's my son. He's God's child. Surely, He will save Mateo."

Her love for God was evident in every word she spoke. I had never met someone with a faith like Isabella's. Glancing at the time, I saw I had just over an hour to get back and try to catch Dean. We decided to take a brief walk in the park, savoring the moment a little longer before heading back. Isabella assured me we would return in time, but my ticking watch added a sense of urgency to the stroll.

Pointing out a field where children played baseball, Isabella spoke of how Mateo loved playing baseball with the neighborhood kids after school and that she believed if not soccer, he could've also been the next Joe DiMaggio. She asked if we could stop briefly, and I obliged. I felt it was the right thing to do for a mother whose son's life was in peril—living with the constant, urgent uncertainty every day—waiting and wondering if God would come through.

As we returned to the church, I was torn between admiration for Isabella's steadfast faith and the weight of my doubts. I thanked her for her kindness and the unexpected friendship between us. Before we parted ways, we exchanged information, a simple act that promised to keep our connection alive. It was three-forty-three, and I knew I had to walk steadily to meet Dean. Several blocks later, I arrived with four minutes to spare, my mind still wrestling with my decision of not being able to meet up with Paul.

The receptionist at the desk remembered me and asked, "Miss, did you say you had an appointment with Mr. Scott?"

When she asked if I was there to see Mr. Scott, I must have looked like a deer caught in headlights. I only knew the name Dean, but I assumed that was his last name, so I replied, "Yes, Mr. Dean Scott. I don't have an appointment, but James told me to stop in and speak with Dean. I mean, Mr. Scott." I hoped she would just let me meet him without an official appointment. My fingers and toes were crossed at this point. I needed this interview to land this job. I desperately wanted to be able to call New York my home.

"Sweetie, you should've led with that. Take a seat over there, and I'll let him know he has a visitor," she said, pointing to a small pale green sofa pushed up against a wall across the way.

I sat quietly, waiting. I wasn't one to pray, but at that moment, I asked God selfishly if he would make sure I could at least get an interview. I didn't have many skills for being a columnist, but I had the passion. I wondered if Mr. Scott would take me seriously if I had no real experience. My self-doubt was heavy as I considered my lack of qualifications. Just as I was about to walk out the door, thinking this was all a big mistake, the receptionist called out as she pointed, "Sweetie, if you stay to the right down the hall, then take a quick left; his office is in the corner. Just knock, and good luck."

Slinging my purse strap over my shoulder, I stood up and headed down the hall, taking a quick left. My stomach tightened as I approached Mr. Scott's office. I kept telling myself to breathe. I could see through his glass door. He walked back and forth, peering out a large glass window overlooking the city. My palms were sweaty. The thought of shaking this man with sweaty palms made me want to throw up. This was my moment, and yet my feet stood in the same spot for nearly thirty seconds before he finally caught notice of me, acknowledging my presence.

"Walking over toward the door, he swung it wide open and said, "Come in," with his arm extended toward his desk.

As I passed him, I nervously wiped my hands on the sides of my dress, hoping he hadn't noticed. Every inch of my body was drenched in sweat. My knees felt weak, and my mouth was parched. Could I even speak? My heart was thumping, and I kept reminding myself to stay calm. Just breathe, Mary. Breathe. I couldn't help but wonder what I had gotten myself into. Was this the right decision? Was I even prepared for this meeting,

"Please, sit," he expressed kindly.

His kindness, especially after our abrupt phone call, caught me off guard, and his unexpected warmth made me question if I was in the right office. Looking around, I could tell by his enormous office and magnificent city view that he was very successful. The walls were adorned with business accolades, including photos of numerous people, some of whom were celebrities. The large windows flooded the room with natural light, with only one light fixture above his desk. The splendor of his office made me want what he had.

Rounding the dark mahogany desk with intricate carvings designed for aesthetics, he pulled out his oversized chair and sat. I was grateful there was no handshake. Pulling out his top drawer on the right side, he sat a dark green bottle of brandy with two Crystal glasses on the desk. The label read: Hennessy. I was sure he needed clarification about who I was and what I came to see him for. This wasn't no Friday night special. I wasn't a call girl, nor was it Friday.

He popped the top off the brandy bottle and began to pour the first glass. As he was about to pour the other, I reached over the glass, stopping him from filling it, and said, "Sir, I'm not sure what's going on here or who you think I am, but I can assure you, you have the wrong lady."

He placed the bottle back on the desk. While screwing the cap back on, he looked directly into my eyes and replied, "I know who you are. You're Mary Gonsalves from Massachusetts. After our brief phone call, I called James. He informed me that you were looking to work here as a columnist and that I should consider hiring you."

At that moment, I was relieved, knowing that James must have spoken highly of me. As Dean put the bottle of Brandy away, he sipped his drink. I wasn't sure if it was because it seemed warm in Dean's office or because I was so nervous that I could feel beads of sweat forming on my forehead. Whatever it was, I was grateful when Dean walked over to his refrigerator and came back with a cold glass bottle of RC cola with the cap popped off.

Tossing the cap in the small wastebasket under his desk, he sat back down, watching me as I took a few sips. The cool liquid soothed my parched throat. I kept it in my hands as I finally formed words, " Dean, I mean…"

He interrupted, "If it's all right with you, I'll call you Mary, and you can call me Dean. This way, neither of us feels uncomfortable, causing us to sweat and have dry mouth." I was utterly embarrassed, and I could tell by the smirk on his face that he knew how nervous I was. He gulped the last of his brandy and asked, "So, do you have any writing experience?"

"I do not. I excelled in literature in school and have always been passionate about writing stories. After graduation, I worked in a factory to support my mother. I have a strong drive, and I'm ready to do whatever it takes to prove my worth to this company, " I declared with conviction. His expression was impenetrable, but I was determined to see if he saw my potential. Either way, I was about to find out.

"Let me be frank, Mary. I receive hundreds of applications annually from men and women wanting a chance at your request. I can't imagine what you can do that a woman with more education can, but James owns this company, and we've been friends for a long time. He's usually good at picking the right people for his company, so I'm willing to take a chance on you, Mary. You start in a week. I can start you off at one hundred and thirty-five dollars a week.

After a month, if newspaper sales increase, we can talk about increasing your pay. I will have my receptionist get all your information for me. I will contact you soon with your first assignment. Do you have any questions for me?"

Despite having several questions, I was too delighted to think of any. Instead, I nodded and said, "I can't think of any at the moment, but I want to express my gratitude for this opportunity. I promise I won't disappoint you."

We both stood at the same time. Dean walked over, shook my hand, and replied, "Many have said the exact words, yet they are no longer employed here. Let's hope you get to stay."

As we parted ways, his comment left a lump in my throat, but I chose not to let it affect me. Stepping out of the building, I was greeted by a brighter world, with birds singing their praises. I felt empowered as I was on top of the world. I couldn't wait to share this feeling with my mother. With several blocks to walk back to the hotel, I knew I would need something refreshing to stay hydrated, so I briefly stopped at a charming Italian pizza joint to use the ladies' room and grab a cold drink.

Twenty-two minutes later, I arrived at the hotel. It was now five-thirty. I stopped at the front desk to ask if there were any messages for me. I knew there wouldn't be, but it made me feel important to ask. Sergio greeted me warmly and said, " Yes, I have one message for you."

"Really," I asked, confused and surprised.

Sergio pointed toward the hotel lounge. Turning around, I tried to figure out what I was supposed to be looking at when I spotted Paul across the room.

"Sergio, when did he get here? I know he stopped working at four," I asked, shocked that he had returned. My heart skipped a beat as I saw him. A mix of surprise and something else I couldn't quite place had me giddy.

"Mary, you're correct. His shift ended at four, but he hadn't left. He's been here the entire time. He didn't tell you that he..."

Sergio took a moment and paused before continuing what he was about to tell me. "Forgive me. It is not my place to divulge his business. Paul is my employee, and he does a fine job here. The guests like him. I would not want to lose him because I spoke out of turn about his business," he confessed.

His cryptic conversation made me curious about Paul, but I respected him for not divulging his employee's business. I thanked Sergio and then headed over toward Paul. He was not in his work uniform but was dressed in a way that caught my eye. He stirred in me a feeling that I hadn't experienced since my school days, which was strange given my age. My past relationships were so short-lived that I had never even experienced what it was like to kiss someone.

Paul rose from his seat and strode toward me, his confidant gait drawing my attention. His choice of attire, a striking red Cuban-collar shirt, black trousers, and polished black penny loafers, exuded a self-assured charm that I found appealing. His hair neatly parted to the right, and his captivating smile further accentuated his confidence. In his presence, I felt we were the sole inhabitants of the lobby, the rest of the world fading into insignificance.

We stopped in front of each other, only a few feet apart. I could smell his cologne. The aroma reminded me of a sweet whiskey—not intense yet captivating. I, on the other hand, reeked of sweat and desperation—embarrassing, to say the least. I didn't expect to find Paul in the lobby; nevertheless, I met up with him, hoping he wouldn't mention my look or smell.

"Mary, it's so good to see you. Would you like to sit or go somewhere to talk?"

Despite my immediate priorities, I was determined to set things right with Paul. The urge to share the good news with my mother and the need to freshen up and change were pressing, but I couldn't bear to dismiss Paul again, who had waited for me. "Yes, I would, but...." Something inside me told me to be honest with him—to say I had a few things I needed to do first. Maybe he would understand.

"It's okay, Mary. If you have some other prior engagement, we can catch up another time," he said reassuringly, his face betraying a hint of disappointment.

"No, Paul, it's not that at all. I wanted to call my mother and share some exciting news with her, and I don't think I can wait until tomorrow if I'm, to be honest. I'd also like the chance to freshen up a bit. Being outside most of the day, walking in the city doesn't leave you so fresh, if you know what I mean," I replied with a half smile.

"Oh yes. I'm so sorry. I didn't even stop to think you'd been gone all day. You must be exhausted. Like I said, we can catch up another time."

"No, I'd like to sit and chat. Can you give me thirty minutes?" I pleaded, a sense of anticipation in my voice.

"Hold on one second," he said as he walked to the bar. Grabbing a cocktail napkin and pen, he jotted down something before returning it to me.

Handing me the napkin, my fingers brushed his hand ever so slightly, causing excitement and nervousness to flood my body. I could feel little beads of sweat start to form on the back of my neck. I wasn't sure if it was from all the running around I did today or from Paul's skin touching mine; either way, I needed to hurry along. I looked down at the napkin. There, he wrote down his room number.

"I figured I'd give you the option. If you want to come by and talk, or if you feel more comfortable, we can meet in the lobby. Maybe grab a bite to eat. Whatever is good for you. I'll be waiting," he said as he walked away.

Wait, what? I watched him walk away, trying to understand why he had a room number. Does he live here? Was that what Sergio was going to tell me? So, if that's correct, he wasn't waiting for me in the lobby all that time. The plot thickened. I was more curious now than ever to find out Paul's story.

Walking over to the other side of the hotel lobby, I dialed my mother and waited. Three rings was all it took for the sweetest voice to answer, "Hello."

"Hi, it's Mary," I responded with excitement.

"Mary, is everything okay? It's not Sunday," she asked with worry in her voice.

"Yes, I just couldn't wait until Sunday to tell you the good news. I got a job at the New York Herald Tribune. James, whom I met on the bus ride here, gave me his business card. He owns the newspaper. He told me to see this guy whose name is Dean. He's his VP. At first, he brushed me off, but I was determined to land this job. I'm not going to lie; it was a little intimidating, yet exciting. I start next week. The pay is decent. Dean said if newspaper sales increase, he could bump my pay."

My mother heard the excitement in my voice as I rambled everything in one fast swoop, ensuring I didn't miss anything. Even though we were on the phone, I knew she was smiling big from the news I had just shared.

"That's wonderful, Mary. I'm happy for you. You're going to do great! Are you settling in okay? Is the hotel treating you nicely?" she asked, checking I wasn't keeping anything from her.

"Yes, I'm doing fine. I'm still alive. The hotel manager, Sergio, has been charming. He's always willing to help and has an inviting smile that instantly puts you at ease. You'd like him. I've only had a few encounters with a few people, and they have been pleasant. I'll try to call as often as possible, but if I can't, I promise to write to you."

"That will be just fine, Mary. I'm going to let you go for now; I'm in the middle of finishing up dinner. I love you, and you be safe."

"I will, Mother. I love you too."

After I ended the phone call with my mother, I returned to my room. As I looked for clothes to wear, I checked the time on my watch. Eleven minutes was all I had to get ready, yet I was determined to look my best, so I chose my outfit carefully—black cigarette pants, a light pink silk blouse, and black buckle Mary Janes. After touching up my face and hair, I sprayed myself with a light perfume before jumping into the elevator to meet Paul with three minutes to spare.

As I passed Sergio's desk, I politely asked, "Could you ring Paul for me?"

Surprised by my request, Sergio said, "Sure, Mary. Would you like me to relay a message, or would you like to speak to him yourself?"

Pointing toward the lounge, I replied, "Please let Paul know I'll be waiting over there, and don't keep a lady waiting too long," adding a playful wink as I walked away. I couldn't resist teasing Sergio a little, and I could tell by his smile that he found humor in my response.

As I sat nervously, my self-conscious thoughts echoing in the silence waiting on Paul, I opened my purse and pulled out my small compact mirror. Checking my appearance, I thought I looked pretty good for someone pressed for time. As I tossed my mirror back into my purse, I heard the elevator bell ding and the doors open. I watched as Paul stepped out. I didn't know what it was, but something about him made me smile and experience a feeling I had never felt. A feeling that enveloped me like a warm, cozy blanket on a cold winter's night.

His stride, reminiscent of Clark Gable, exuded a commanding presence. As he drew closer, I tried to maintain my composure, but the flutter in my stomach betrayed my anticipation. I rose to my feet, my heart pounding as he neared. Like a sudden burst of sunlight, his smile lit up the room as he greeted me, "It's a pleasure to see you again, Mary."

The scent of his cologne, a tantalizing blend, drew me in. For a fleeting moment, I imagined what it would feel like to be in his arms. Quickly shaking off the fantasy, I replied," It's wonderful to see you too, Paul."

"Would you like to go somewhere or just sit here and talk," he asked, pointing toward two empty chairs near the bar.

"It doesn't matter to me," I answered, secretly hoping he would be a gentleman and take me to dinner. I was a little hungry and thought a delightful meal with him would be pretty appealing.

"Okay, then, dinner it is. I know of a great place unless you're not hungry. Then we can do something else or stay here—whatever you want."

He started strong and confident, but somewhere, it seemed as if maybe I made him a bit nervous. Trying to ease his mind, I smiled and replied, "Dinner would be lovely, thank you."

Paul and I decided to walk several blocks, seeing that the temperature had dropped and a warm but comfortable breeze filled the air. He offered to pay for a cab, but I said I would rather walk to admire the city. He pointed out a few things along the way, including historical facts. He was like my own personal tour guide. I found it quite amusing and helpful. Twelve minutes later, we arrived at a restaurant called China Peace, which was located on West Forty-Forth St and the corner of Broadway.

Paul opened the door like a gentleman, allowing me to enter first. We stepped aside, letting other patrons leave as we waited to be seated. A beautiful Chinese lady who looked to be in her early twenties greeted us. "Hello, welcome to China Peace. Will it just be the two of you?" she asked.

"Yes, please, and if it's no trouble, would it be possible to get a table toward the back," Paul inquired in a charming voice.

The young lady batted her lashes, tossed her long jet, smooth, silky hair over her left shoulder, and replied, "Yes, sir, no bother at all. Come, follow me."

With two menus in her hand, she led us toward the back corner, away from other guests. Paul walked around toward my chair, pulling it out for me. The young lady informed us that our waitress would be at our table shortly. I took in the atmosphere while we waited. The place was stunning.

We sat at a round table draped with a white linen cloth that had already been set up with dinnerware: plates with gold around the rim, silverware, and a napkin shaped into a swan for eye-catching esthetics. Above each table hung lanterns with red tassels, giving just the proper lighting. The restaurant was impeccable, carefully considering every detail to make customers feel special.

After our waitress Ying took our order, I initiated a conversation with the apology I felt Paul deserved. Nervous, I fidgeted with my purse strap, which lay across my lap, as I said, " Please let me start by apologizing for my behavior when we first met. Looking back, I understand that I could've handled it better. I didn't mean to make you feel so bad that you thought you needed to write me a note. I was taken aback. I mean, I have to know, do you always kiss every woman's hand you meet?"

He laughed. I laughed with him, not knowing why he was laughing. Just as he was about to reply to my question, the waitress came over with our dinner, which looked amazing and smelled delicious. Making sure we had everything we needed, she asked, "Does everything look good? Do you need anything?"

"Mary, do you need anything," Paul Asked.

"Looking toward him and then Ying, I smiled and replied, "No, I'm good. This looks amazing."

Topping off our drinks, she said, "Enjoy," before walking away.

I wasn't sure if Paul would answer my question, but I was too hungry to worry about that. The food smelled terrific, making my mouth water. Several bites in, Pual placed his fork on his dish and said, "Okay, back to your question, Mary. No, I don't make it a habit of kissing women I meet on the hand. When I kissed yours, I did that without thinking. I was just as shocked as you were, and again, I'm sorry."

I genuinely believed him and accepted his apology. Throughout dinner, we shared little things about ourselves with each other. I told him why I came to New York and how I just landed a job, which I was ecstatic about. He congratulated me and said I would excel in my new endeavor even though he didn't know me, which was kind. Paul explained that he was originally from Washington State and moved to Montana, but he needed a change, so he decided to come to New York.

"So, How long have you been working at the hotel?" I asked.

"I've been working there for about six months. The pay is decent, but I'm unsure if New York will be my permanent home or if I'll find myself back in Montana. What about you, Mary? Can you see yourself here permanently?"

"Honestly, I don't know what tomorrow will bring, never mind the future. I'm focused on my career and don't need any distractions. I can't afford to mess this up."

I felt terrible being so blunt, but I needed him to know I wasn't looking for Casanova. The only thing I could offer him was friendship. His face, a constant smile, now presented an unmistakable disappointment. Our waitress, Ying, returned to provide us with dessert, but neither of us could imagine eating anymore as we were both full. Instead, Paul, in his usual polite manner, asked for the check.

"Thank you for dining with us. I hope everything was satisfying. I will leave this with you, and you can go to the register when you're ready. There is no rush. Have a fantastic night," Ying said as she walked away.

Paul took the check and handed me one of the two fortune cookies Ying left us. I was never big on fortune cookies, but I at least wanted to see what my fortune said. Tearing the package open, I crushed the cookie and unfolded the fortune. Paul did the same.

"What does yours say, Mary?" Paul asked.

I felt mine fit my current situation, so I didn't mind reading it. "It reads, Success lies in the hands of those who want it."

"Hey, that's perfect, Mary," Paul exclaimed.

"Okay, now read yours, Paul," I said with a hint of excitement in my voice, eager to hear what this tiny slip of paper had in store for him.

"Mine isn't as good as yours. It's not worth reading," he declared while crumpling it up and leaving it on the table before getting up to pull out my chair.

I didn't press the issue, but I did take it off the table and tuck it in my purse without him noticing. I should've left it behind, but I couldn't. After Paul paid for our dinner, we headed back toward the hotel. He asked if I wanted to take a stroll, but I was getting tired, and it was after eight o'clock. We spoke a little bit more, but it had nothing to do with our lives per se; it had more to do with specific places in New York.

When we returned, Paul walked me to my room like a gentleman, and we parted ways, but not before asking me, "Mary, I was wondering if you would like to go out sometime again?"

I was torn. I did enjoy myself, yet I didn't want him to think this would turn into some romantic love story. I'm no Judy Garland trying to fall in love with the neighbor in the movie

Meet Me in St. Loius, which, by the title, doesn't take place in New York. However, I liked his company and friendship, so I clarified by saying, "I would but as friends."

He accepted my offer, and from then on, we became friends.

Chapter Six

Several weeks have passed since I arrived in New York, and while my job has been going well, my friendship with Paul has grown. We've been out several times, enjoying each other's company. Dean called me today, letting me know he was giving me an exclusive to write. I hoped it would be more interesting than the articles I've written for weeks. I was tired of writing tips on how to get stains out of slacks or the best recipe to make Chicken Ala King. I felt a surge of confidence, knowing it was my time to shine. I was excited. Today would be a great day, and I was excited to head to work.

As I quickly exited the hotel lobby, I unexpectedly bumped into Paul. I informed him about my time constraint—that I had only twenty minutes to reach work. He empathized with my situation and kept our conversation brief, but not before revealing a surprise he had in store for me. I agreed to meet him in the hotel lobby at seven, intrigued by what he had planned.

Arriving at Dean's office just a minute before our scheduled meeting, I sat across his desk as he engaged in a phone call. The anticipation of this exclusive writing opportunity was intense, filling me with thrilling excitement and nervousness. It was hard not to overhear parts of Dean's conversation, but by the sound of it, someone was about to get fired. Hanging up the phone, he looked me straight in the face and said, "I'm counting on you, Mary."

I wasn't exactly sure what Dean was talking about, but I was sure he was about to tell me. My palms were sweaty, but I nodded confidently as I replied, "Whatever you need, Dean, I'm your gal." I couldn't believe I said, I'm your gal. Who speaks like that to their boss? I thought.

"Listen, I just got word that the big shot who owns TV Guide is about to release the first issue this Friday, and you know who they are featuring on the cover? Do you?" Dean asked with great anxiety.

"Um, I...." He didn't give me time to even guess before interrupting me.

"No, you don't. That was a rhetorical question. Let me tell you: Lucille Ball, the queen of comedy, and her Cuban husband Desi Arnaz's baby will be on it. That's right, Desi Arnaz Jr. So, I need you to write the best article. We are going to put it out into the world a day early. We've never been ahead in all my years, but this time we will be. You bring me something good in twelve hours, I mean good, and I'll give you the front page."

The weight of Dean's words hung in the air, the gravity of the task settling heavily on my shoulders. I couldn't fail. Standing up confidently, I assured him I would come through and wouldn't let him down. As he walked me out, he said, "I'll expect it within twelve hours, Mary." My determination was profound, and I could see Dean was serious about this piece. I was committed to meeting the deadline, no matter what.

"There's a small office that no one uses, Mary. It's yours," he said.

I was over the moon as I swiftly went from Dean's office to mine. I had been writing in the conference room on the second floor since starting here, but now my very own office. I couldn't believe it. I was moving up in the world. Opening the door, I looked around. Of course, it looked nothing like Dean's, but I didn't care. The excitement of having my own space was profound. As silly as that sounded, I felt like I was getting somewhere in my career.

What was once a hole in the wall had become a place for potential. The small wooden desk, chair, typewriter, paper, and pen were no longer objects but tools for my craft. Dean's words echoed in my mind- the front page. This was no longer just a job. It was a space where my dreams could come true. With my knowledge of Lucille Ball and Desi Arnaz, I was confident in my ability to craft a story that would enthrall readers. I was ready to showcase my writing skills.

I knew I had a deadline to meet, but I also needed to leave the office for just a bit, so I returned to talk with Dean. I informed him I'd be back shortly. He again expressed the importance of this piece, but I assured him I had it under control. Agreeing with my request, I headed for the hotel to let Paul know that the surprise would have to be postponed and hoped he would understand. When I arrived, I sought out Sergio at the front desk, hoping he could guide me to Paul, who had just finished his shift. Sergio informed me that Paul had retired to his room.

Quickly entering the elevator, I ascended to the fourth floor. The doors opened, and I jumped out, making my way three doors down, knocking on Paul's door. He answered the door, wearing no shirt. My throat formed a lump. My eyes widen without thought. Nonchalantly, he asked, "Hey Mary, What's up? I didn't expect us to meet for another hour or so."

My mind was a whirlwind of conflicting thoughts. I've been trying to keep my friendship platonic with Paul, yet he answered the door .... Mary, stop, I tell myself, so my thoughts don't wander to a forbidden place where they shouldn't. Focusing my eyes on Paul, I answer, "I hate to do this, Paul, but can I take a raincheck tonight? I wouldn't do this to you if it weren't imperative, but my boss just dropped this big story on me that I need to finish in twelve hours. He will give me the front page if I come through as he's expecting. Do you know what this means?" I blurted out, my voice trembling with anxiety.

"It's going to be alright, Mary. Take a deep breath before you pass out. I've never seen you like this. I mean, you've written some good columns before. What's the big deal?" he asked, dumbfounded.

"What the big deal? Did you not hear me when I said the front page!" I exclaimed.

"Yes, I heard you. I'm just saying you got this. What can I do?"

Trying to stay focused seemed hard, as Paul was still half-naked in the doorway of his room. Without hesitation, I replied, "What you can do is put a shirt on, please. I'm trying to have a meaningful conversation with you, and you're half-naked. Also, you can say, "Mary, it's okay for us to reschedule for tonight."

He laughed as he walked over to his bed, grabbed his t-shirt, and slid it over his head, covering what God created perfectly. "Is this better?"

"Yes, it is. You've never seen me answering the door with my blouse off, have you?" I interjected before he could say something wise, simply putting my hand up.

"Mary, I apologize, but to be fair, I didn't know you'd be the one on the other side of the door when I opened it," He stated with that smile that drove me crazy.

Changing the course of our conversation, I asked, "So you're okay with us doing whatever you had planned for tonight?"

"Of course it is. Now, go write something the world will be talking about for days," he said, encouraging me to be great.

"Thanks, Paul," I replied while waving as I hurried toward the elevator.

I stopped at the little Italian pizza place a block from my work. I didn't have time to dine in, so I took the pizza to go. The lady behind the counter was very accommodating. She made sure I had a paper plate and some extra napkins. I didn't need a drink.

I arrived back at work just before seven-thirty and now had under nine hours to get this article written and turned in. Making my way toward my office, I passed Dean as he was shutting off his light to head home. While carrying his briefcase in his left, he raised his right arm, pointing toward me, and said, "You got this, Mary," his understanding of my situation was a testament to the camaraderie we shared in our workplace.

There was nothing like unmeasurable amounts of pressure to get the job done, and I had no time to waste. I gave myself fifteen minutes to eat before diving into my work. Sliding a sheet of paper in my typewriter, I began. The headline and article would read,

Queen of Comedy Lucille Ball and Cuban Musician Husband Desi Arnaz, Light Up The World with Baby Desi Arnaz Jr. on TV Guide's First Issue cover, a special edition that will delve into the lives and careers of these iconic figures.

Yes, you heard that right. The first issue will feature the son of TV star Lucille Ball and real-life husband Desi Arnaz Sr. Mrs. Ball began her career at eighteen when she landed work as a model, yet it didn't take long for her to perform on Broadway using the stage name Diane Belmont. One of her significant roles which gained her recognition was a play called **Stage Door**. *She has had many films uncredited, yet has risen to fame with her TV show, I Love Lucy.*

Desi Arnaz began his career playing the conga drum and singing. His big break came when Xavier Cugat saw Desi performing and offered him a gig touring with his Orchestra. Their early careers set the stage for their future success. As his recognition grew with audiences, Desi

formed his band, the Desi Arnaz Orchestra. Over the next couple of years, Desi starred on Broadway and hit the big screen in California, where he soon met Lucy.

On November 30, 1940, the two eloped. Three years later, Desi was drafted for war. However, after completing his training, he was limited to the United States Army due to injuries. Therefore, he was assigned to USO in Birmingham, where, after two years, seven months, and four days, he was awarded the Army Good Conduct Medal, the American Campaign Medal, and the World War Two Victory Medal. This service significantly influenced his career.

*This is Lucy and Desi's second child together. Their daughter Lucie Arnaz was born a year and a half earlier. While juggling being a wife and mother to two precious children, Lucy and Desi find time for each other while working together on the hit show **I Love Lucy**. The show first gained attention when Lucy played Liz Cooper on a radio talk show called My Favorite Husband. CBS wanted to develop it for TV production, but Lucy wouldn't do the show if her real-life husband Desi could be with her. CBS wasn't impressed by the pilot, so Lucy and Desi took their show on the road, facing numerous challenges, but it was successful.*

*It wasn't until 1951, two years ago, that CBS realized their mistake. Luci and Desi own their own production company, Desilu, and their show has succeeded. CBS put **I Love Lucy** in their line-up on October 15, 1951, and it's been a hit since. The birth of Desi Arnaz Jr was a pivotal moment in the show, incorporated into the episode **Lucy Goes to the Hospital,** Season Two, Episode Sixteen, where Lucy gives birth to little Ricky Ricardo.*

The first issue of Baby Desi Arnaz Jr. will hit stands on April 3rd. It will also feature a picture of his famous mother, Lucille Ball.

I felt good about the article and was ready to lay it on Dean's desk. It took just over five hours and several mistakes to complete. Would it be enough for the front page? I won't know until tomorrow. I needed to get back to the hotel for some much-needed rest. Shutting off the light in my office, I placed my work on Dean's desk and rode the elevator to the lobby.

As I stepped off the elevator, minimal lighting in the lobby made it hard to see. A large glass window shined light, giving me a path toward the door. It was now close to one in the morning, and walking several blocks toward the hotel wasn't my best option. I figured I'd hail a cab to be on the safe side. With a few feet left exiting the building, I noticed a shadowy figure sitting in one of the chairs near the receptionist's desk.

I couldn't determine who it was, so I hollered, "I'm not alone."

"Neither am I now that you are here," a voice called out.

Approaching slowly, I walked toward the large glass window where the moon lit up part of the room. Getting closer, I shook my head and said, "How did you get in here? And why are you here, Paul?"

"It's nice to see you too, Mary," he amusedly answered.

"I mean, it's not that I'm not happy to see you, but why are you here, and who let you in?" I asked, confused about the situation at hand.

"I got to thinking. You said it would be late before you got back to the hotel, and I didn't want you to have to walk alone or even take a cab this late at night, so I came here waiting for you. Dean let me in and said I could wait for you in the lobby."

"Wait, what? How long have you been here? What if I was still working? What if I didn't get done for another three hours? Then what?" I asked.

He laughed for a few seconds, shaking his head before saying, "Mary, that's a lot of what-ifs. I don't think any of that matters now. What matters is that I'm here to escort you back to the hotel safely," he replied, his protective gesture of looping his arm through mine like a chaperon at a dance, comforting me.

I knew it was too late to bother with semantics, so I obliged, putting my arm through his as we walked out of the building. "What about the doors? I don't have a key." I asked, my confusion adding a layer of intrigue to the situation.

"Dean said they would automatically lock behind us," Paul stated, his voice carrying a tone of reassurance that washed over me, making me feel secure.

Neither of us spoke much on the way back. We enjoyed the walk and each other's company, with our connection growing more robust with each step. Two blocks from the hotel, we passed a man lying on a piece of cardboard with newspapers draped over his head. My heart was broken. This is someone's child. Grown, but still someone's child. Paul took notice of my face. I wanted to say something, but what?

When we arrived at the hotel, Paul asked if I would sit in one of the lobby chairs for just a few minutes. I wasn't sure what he was doing or if he realized how tired I was, but I did as he asked.I stared at the beautiful gold-adorned clock on the wall across from me. Its rhythmic ticking filled the air, a constant reminder of the passing of time. The more I stared, the heavier my eyes became, the weight of the night settling on my shoulders. It wasn't until I heard Sergio's familiar voice call out, "Mary, is that you, dear?" That I snapped out of it.

Standing up, I walked over to Sergio, who was wiping down the marble counter in front of him. Sergio was more than a concierge manager; he had become a friend. "Hello, Sergio," I greeted him warmly.

"It's late, Mary. Is everything okay? Was there something you needed?" he asked.

"No. I'm just waiting for Paul to come back. I'm unsure where he went, but he assured me he would return momentarily."

And just like that, Paul came around the corner with a small gray blanket and a bag. "Hey, Sergio, I hope you don't mind. I grabbed a few leftovers. Just take it out of my next check," he stated, showing him what he had.

"Paul, don't worry about it. I'll use it as a write-off. The hotel can afford it," Sergio reassured him with a smile.

With the blanket rolled up under Paul's arm and the bag in his left hand, he extended out his right hand, and without hesitation, I accepted his offer. I felt safe with him. I felt as if our hands fit perfectly together. As we walked, I thought about how much I wanted Paul as more than just a friend, but I knew he wasn't part of my plans. I needed to stay focused. There was no future for us.

Paul realized I was deep in thought when I wasn't talking and asked, "Mary, what's running through that beautiful mind of yours?"

Shaking my head, I replied, "I'm just tired. It's been a long day, and it's past my bedtime."

He didn't question my answer; he just apologized for keeping me up with him. I expressed that it was okay and that there was no need to apologize. We made it back to where the man was lying on the ground. Bending down, Paul called out, "Sir, I have a blanket and some food for you."

He didn't move nor acknowledge our existence. Paul called out to him again, but this time, reaching out with his hand, he nudged the man., "Get down, the man yelled as he grabbed Paul and threw him toward the ground. I quickly jumped back in fear for my safety, but Paul just stayed on the ground, whispering to the man, "I got you. I'll follow your lead."

After a few tense moments, they both got up as if nothing had happened. Paul saluted the man, thanked him for his service, and handed him the bag with food and a blanket. The man's demeanor softened, saying, "That was close. We need to have each other's back. It was a great honor serving with you," before leaving the cardboard and newspapers behind. His words carried a weight of gratitude that touched us both.

Emotions surged through me, a sudden whirlwind of events. It all unfolded in a blur, yet the outcome was unexpectedly beautiful. Paul's hand reached for mine, his voice breaking the chaos, "Are you okay, Mary?"

"I'm okay. I'm glad you weren't hurt trying to help him, " I replied.

"This isn't my first time in this situation," he proclaimed.

As we returned to the hotel, Paul opened up about his brother's struggles. Harry and he both served in the Army during World War Two, and the war had left its mark. "Harry has never been the same since he came home. His wife Elsie has called me crying and worried about him. She said he sometimes woke up in cold sweats, just yelling. It would frighten her," Paul explained, his voice heavy with concern for his brother and sister-in-law. His story underscored the need to understand and empathize with the experiences of war veterans.

As far as I knew, no one in my family had served, but I've always had the utmost respect for those who do and their families. Although it was extremely late, I felt I had a second wind and wanted to hear more about Paul's life, but I knew I needed to go to bed. I had to return to work in less than six hours. Paul was kind enough to walk me to my hotel room, where we parted ways, but not before leaning in to hug me goodnight. "I figured a friendly hug goodnight would be acceptable, Mary," he stated with a slight smile, hoping I would agree.

"Yes, Paul, that was fine. Have a good night, and I'll catch up with you tomorrow," I said before closing the door.

Kicking off my shoes, I slithered into the bathroom to brush my teeth, toss on my nightgown, and crawl into bed. I didn't bother turning on the TV; instead, I let the sounds of the city lull me to sleep.

Chapter Seven

I awoke the following day to the phone ringing. Sergio informed me that Dean was expecting me in the office and that if I wanted to keep my job, I'd better be there immediately. I wasted no time getting dressed and out the door. Quickly jumping out of the elevator, I interlaced with several guests checking in. Because I was so pressured for time, I didn't even bother to greet Sergio or Paul, who was ten feet away from me. Nope, the only thing that mattered was me keeping my job.

I hustled several blocks, my breath coming in ragged gasps, each a sharp reminder of my physical exertion. I weaved in and out of people on the streets, feeling the heat of their bodies as I tried not to pass out. I could feel my heart beating in my throat, a powerful rhythm matching my pace's urgency. I rounded the corner so fast that as I approached the office building, I ran smack into the glass door when a gentleman from the second-floor billing department came out from the other side. I could feel blood trickling from my nose down to my chin.

"Oh my gosh! Are you all right?" The voice asked, sounding faint.

My eyes jolted in my head, and my vision blurred for a few seconds. I felt someone touching my arm, but I couldn't focus yet. I heard the voice calling out and asking for a napkin from a distance. Finally, my vision became clear again. Tim, who accidentally hit me with the door, handed me several napkins while continuously apologizing. I explained to him that it was partly my fault as I was rushing and should've paid more attention. Once my nose stopped bleeding, I felt relieved and parted ways, expressing my heartfelt thanks to Tim for his quick assistance as I hurried to the lady's room.

I quickly looked in the mirror and thought, it is what it is, Mary. Just get to Dean's office. Tossing the bloody napkin in the trash, I grabbed a paper towel, wetted half of it, wiped the dried blood off my face, and threw that, too, before heading to find out my fate. I was so disheveled, and felt a little queasy, but I suppressed that feeling way down. The last thing I needed was to throw up while listening to Dean chew me out.

Stopping at the entrance of Dean's door, I brushed the strands of hair away from my face, straightened my blouse, took a deep breath, and knocked. He tells me to enter. I don't bother to sit, not knowing if I'll still have my job. His desk is in disarray, with several papers scattered everywhere. "Mary, you know I expected you here on time, right?" he asked.

His voice is stern, like that of a father scolding his child. As I was about to reply to his question, he noticed my blouse had droplets of dried blood and asked, "What happened?"

"Oh, this," I pointed to my blouse. "It's nothing. I just got hit in the face with a door. I'm fine."

His eyebrows raised as he replied, "Are you sure, Mary? Is this why you were late?"

"No. This had nothing to do with me being late, although getting hit in the face by a door did slow me down a few minutes," I replied with a slight smile, hoping he would have a little sympathy.

"Well, as long as you're okay with it, we can proceed. We have some things to discuss about your future here."

I wasn't okay. My head was splitting, and I was still nauseous, but I figured if I was going to get fired, I wanted it to be quick and painless. I had already endured enough pain this morning. He asked me to take a seat, which I complied. Mostly because I felt dizzy. I was pretty sure I had a concussion. I didn't wait for him to give me the third degree in punctuality. I figured I'd beat him to the punch and suffer the consequences.

"Sir, If I may. What I'm about to say isn't me making an excuse. This is me justifying why I overslept. Last night, I worked my tail off, making sure I wrote an article fit for the front page. Did I? I feel I did, but you call the shots at the end of the day. I want to say that although I may disagree with you letting me go, I have worked hard for you in the past couple of months. I love what I do, but I can't, nor will I beg you to keep my job, so go ahead. Let's get this over with."

He stood up, walked toward the window, looked at the city, and said, "You know what I love about this city? I'll tell you, Mary. There are opportunities for so many seeking a chance to make a difference. I've been doing this for a long time, and you know what? I can spot talent. I can also spot conviction, passion, and hard-working individuals who hunger for a chance at success. You? Boy, I thought I had you pegged from the first moment I saw you.

You have all those qualities, Mary. That's precisely why you are getting the front page. Your drive, passion, and storytelling are exactly what this newspaper company has been looking for. I loved your article. So this is what I'm going to do for you. You'll continue writing small puff pieces for me to fill on page ten. You know, the usual recipes, housekeeping tips, best appliances for the everyday housewife, those kind of things."

When he first opened his mouth, I thought I was fired, but then he gave me the front page and praised me. But now this? I didn't want to assume anything, so I waited for him to continue. Although it was only seconds before he continued, the following pause felt like a lifetime.

Dean continued, "I'm going to bump your pay to seven cents more an article, which, at one article a day Monday through Friday, will increase your pay by thirty-five cents. And there's one more thing: anytime there's a big story to be told, you're my gal. That's right, front page. How's that sound?"

It took every ounce of self-control not to leap out of the chair, rush toward Dean, and embrace him. What held me back, you wonder? I sensed it was a tad inappropriate. So I composed myself and replied, " This morning, I thought I had lost my chance here, and then this! I can't express my gratitude enough, sir."

I started to sweat profusely. I wasn't sure if it was from the excitement or me having a concussion. Either way, I was over the moon. Before I left Dean's office, he said that even though I was late coming in, he had no intentions of letting me go. I asked him why he would leave me a message like that. His response was he likes to keep his people on their toes. Although I felt it was unnecessary and somewhat cruel, I let it go. I didn't care. I was ecstatic and felt like I was on cloud nine, floating in a sea of joy.

Arriving at the hotel, I stopped by the desk and asked Sergio if he had some aspirin. I was feeling quite unwell, with a pounding headache and a queasy stomach. He handed me a small bottle he had behind the counter and told me to keep it and that he had more in the office. He also noticed my blouse and asked if I was all right. I didn't get into all the details, but I assured him I was okay.

When I reached my room, I went into the bathroom, filled a glass of warm water, not waiting for it to get cold, and swallowed the aspirin. I just wanted to get undressed, take a relaxing bath, and crawl into bed. It was just before noon, and I still felt under the weather, even after soaking in the bathtub. Crawling under the covers, I turned on the TV, letting the sound lull me to sleep, hoping I'd feel better when I awoke later. It didn't feel like I was asleep long when I was awakened by someone pounding on the door. I checked the time, and four hours had already passed. Man, that knock in the face did a number on me. I thought.

I yelled, "Be there in a minute," as I grabbed my silk robe and tied it around my waist before opening the door.

On the other side of the door stood Paul. Before I could speak, he asked, in a problematic tone, "Mary, Are you okay? I saw you come back a while ago, but I was with several guests and couldn't get away. You looked disheveled, and when I asked Sergio if he had spoken to you, he told me you weren't feeling good. He didn't elaborate any more than that."

The way Paul expressed his concern, you would have thought someone had told him I got into a fight with a bobcat. It was just a glass door, but he didn't need to know all the details as it was embarrassing enough. " Yes, Paul, I'm fine. I was napping. I didn't realize I slept for so long. I'm glad you came by to check on me. I might have slept until tomorrow," I said, appreciating his concern.

"So, what happened at work," he asked, eager to hear how my article went.

"I'd invite you in to tell you all about it, but I'm not dressed," I pointed out.

"Oh, yeah, right. I'm sorry. How about you get ready? I'll pick you up in an hour. You still owe me that raincheck. We can meet in the lobby if you feel up to it."

"Yes, that will be just fine," I replied, waving him to go so I could close the door.

"Perfect," he replied with a cheesy grin before walking away.

With a limited wardrobe, I had wished I had gone shopping at least once since I'd been in New York, but that didn't matter. What mattered was finding something to wear now. After pondering for a few minutes, I slipped on my navy blue-white polka dot dress and Mary Jane flats. I carefully pulled up half my hair and clipped it back, allowing me to wear my small heart-shaped pearl earrings. They always seemed to compliment the dress perfectly. While I'm not one for heavy makeup, I added a touch of rose blush to my cheeks and a hint of rose red lipstick, a recent purchase from Avon.

Before leaving my room and heading for the elevator, I re-checked myself one last time, ensuring I didn't accidentally have lipstick on my teeth or too much blush. My mother always said you can tell what a woman thinks of herself based on how much make-up she wears. She also told me I had natural beauty and radiant skin that most Hollywood actresses would kill for. I was grateful for her influence on my self-perception.

Sliding my watch on, I grabbed my purse and approached the elevator. It was there that Isabella, whom I met a while ago at St. Patrick Cathedral, came walking toward me. I greeted her and asked if Mateo was okay. She said she wanted to tell me the great news in person.

With tears of joy streaming down Isabella's face, she shared, "Oh, Mary, God heard, and he answered my prayers. Matoe is getting better. He still has a long road ahead, but the doctors said it's a miracle. I told them that God's grace and mercy had prevailed."

Opening my purse, I handed her a tissue and replied, "I'm so happy Mateo is getting better, Isabella. I believe he's answered you because of your strong faith in Him."

Isabella wrapped her arms around me. I could feel the power of friendship and love, which made me tear up. When she let go and stepped back, she said, "Wow, you look stunning. I'm guessing I caught you at a bad time. I'm so sorry, Mary."

"I chuckled and replied, "Isabella, don't be foolish. I'm so glad you stopped by to see me. You sharing this wonderful news has made my day. I'm just heading out with a friend. Trust me, he will wait for me." As soon as the word **he** came out of my mouth, I could almost see the spark of curiosity in her eyes, and I knew she would want to know who this man was.

"Mary, I know you must get going, but a man? Oh my, I can't believe what I'm hearing. We need to catch up. I'm free next Saturday in the afternoon. Would that work for you?"

There I went, putting my foot in my mouth. I nodded my head and answered, "Of course. I'd like that. Where would you like to meet?"

"I can meet you at Fanelli Café' around noon if that's good for you," Isabella replied, taking the initiative.

"Yes, that will be perfect," I replied warmly.

We rode the elevator down to the lobby, casually going our separate ways. I strolled toward the front desk, exchanging a few words with Sergio to avoid Isabella seeing Paul. It wasn't about hiding Paul. It was about keeping things light and easy. After my brief chat with Sergio, I went to the bar where Paul awaited me. His patience was a testament to our relaxed relationship.

I couldn't help but notice how Paul's eyes widened with anticipation as he smiled. His neatly combed hair and the crispness of his suit added to his charm. "Wow! You look stunning, Mary," he exclaimed, his eyes lingering on my dress.

"Thank you, Paul. Your kind words always make me feel special," I replied, reciprocating the respect and warmth in our relationship. "You clean up nice, yourself."

Heading from the hotel, Paul opened the door for me like a gentleman. I followed his lead, curious about what he had planned. It was around five in the afternoon, and I was getting hungry. My stomach made noises like two bobcats fighting for their last meal. I was hoping Paul didn't hear, but I got the feeling he did when he said, "I know this small Italian restaurant just south of Little Italy in Chinatown if you'd like to stop there. I've never been. This will be a new place for both of us. I've heard good things about it." The thought of a delicious Italian meal made my stomach growl even louder.

I shrugged and replied, "Sure, if that's what you want."

"I'd say you're hungry from the sounds coming from your stomach, Mary," Paul remarked with a hint of laughter.

I could feel my face turn five shades of red. We both knew my stomach was the master, allowing us to share a light-hearted moment before the evening started. Paul hailed a cab, and we hopped in. Getting to the restaurant took roughly ten minutes, so I decided to share the good news from work with Paul on the ride there. He was genuinely happy for me, saying he knew I'd get the front page. His support was comforting and encouraging.

We arrived at Forlini's, where we were greeted by an Italian gentleman who I could tell came from Italy by his dialect. He sat us in an oversized, deep red high-back booth with a white tablecloth, many wine glasses, and two sets of polished silverware on a napkin. The gold chandeliers with warm, soft lighting hung from the ceiling, cascading a gentle glow over the room. Pictures from Italy adorned the walls, each telling a story. The soft strains of Italian music filled the air, transporting us to the heart of Italy.

A waitress came over and said, "Ciao e benvenuto a Forlini. My name is Gianna, and I'll be taking your order tonight. Can I start you off with some drinks?"

Paul's polite smile indicated he didn't understand Gianna's initial greeting, so I kindly responded, "Un minuto," toward Gianna.

Paul was surprised when I conversed with Gianna in Italian. Before I could explain to Paul what she had said to us in Italian, he looked at me and remarked, "Huh, we are full of surprises, Mary."

Before I responded, Gianna and I laughed. "Surprises, no. I'm Portuguese. Many Italian and Portuguese words have similar roots, so I usually understand what is being said," I explained to Paul.

"Good to know, but I still don't know what she said, Mary."

"Hello and welcome to Forlini, is what she spoke in Italian," I informed him.

Understanding our situation, Gianna quickly reassured us, "I apologize, sir, but the owner requested that we greet patrons in Italian first. You can trust me when I say I'll speak English for the rest of the night while you're dining with us," she said showing respect for our comfort.

Trying to be funny, Paul said, "Gianna, if you'd like to speak in Italian, that is absolutely fine. I have a translator sitting with me. I'm sure by the end of the night, I'll find out she's also a secret agent."

Gianna snickered under her breath as I nudged Paul's arm and said, "Haha. Can we order?"

Paul and I both ordered the Veal Cutlet Parmigiana with a tossed salad and Italian dressing on the side. I've never been big on wine, so I ordered a Shirley Temple, while Paul ordered a Club soda. We made small talk while we waited for our food to arrive.

"So, Paul, I still don't know much about your life before New York." I pointed out, hoping he'd share.

"Yes, this is true. Okay, so what would you like to know, Mary?"

I decided to dig deep into who Paul was before and his life now. "Tell me about your earlier days as a child. You know, your parents, your siblings, what life was like where you were raised, that kind of stuff."

After siping his drink, he began, "All right, if that interests you, but there's not much to tell. My parents were Canadian but moved to Montana before having the twelve of us. Yes, you heard that right. Twelve, but now I have only seven." Paul paused, his eyes reflecting a deep sorrow. It was clear the loss of his siblings had left a profound mark on him.

As I extended my hand across the table, I saw the pain in Paul's eyes. He nodded, his voice heavy with emotion, "The grief never truly fades, no matter how much time passes. I also lost my mother in nineteen twenty-three when I was just twenty- five. It was tough, and I still feel her loss today. She was a true gift from God. Always putting us children first, never complaining, and loving my father with all her heart."

Although Paul's story was heartbreaking, to say the least, I felt moved by his raw vulnerability. As he was about to continue, Gianna came over with our food. It looked delicious. Before we dug in, I asked Paul if he minded if I said Grace. I told him it was a tradition I had with my mother. He smiled and said, "By all means, please. My mother used to have us say, Grace, but that all changed when she died.

Paul and I bowed our heads, and I began, " *Dear Father God, thank you for always being so gracious. May we always humble ourselves and honor you. Please bless the hands that prepared our food. I ask that you continue to heal Paul's heart and remind him that the loved ones he's lost are at peace with you. Amen."* Our shared moment of Grace deepened our emotional connection.

Paul's smile was a welcome sight as we enjoyed our meal. The veal was tender and flavorful, bathed in a rich tomato sauce and melted cheese. At the same time, the salad was a refreshing contrast, crisp and fresh—the combination of flavors and textures made for a delightful dining experience. In between bites, Paul revealed more of his life, making me feel deeply connected with him.

"After losing my mother, four brothers, and one sister, I felt Montana was telling me to get out, or I'd die there like them, so I packed up and left for New York. It's been tough, but I've managed."

I was intrigued by Paul's life in New York, so I asked, "How long have you been here? You said you've been working at the hotel for six months."

"It has been just over five years now," he confessed, his eyes reflecting the memories of his journey from Montana to New York, his struggles, and the new life he built in the bustling city.

Before I could delve deeper into Paul's life, Gianna approached us, asking about our meal and tempting us with dessert. Despite our full stomachs, we shared a slice of New York cheesecake before leaving. It was now past eight, and I was feeling a bit weary, but the thought of a leisurely Saturday ahead, free from work, was a comforting relief. I would wait and see how things played out. Paul pulled out my chair, paid the check, and we left the restaurant, ready to unwind for the night.

Mary's parents from Cape Verde

Family pictures.

Joseph & Dominga Gonsalves
'Circa'1910

'The Rouleau' Family 1910 - Montana Circled is Paul Rouleau – Russ's dad.

'Paul' 1945 – New York

'Paul' 1935

'Mary' 1946 – Connecticut

Mary – 1963

'Buttonwood Park – New Bedford 1958

'Minnie, Russell, Mary'

'Minnie, Janice, Mary, Bea' – 1945

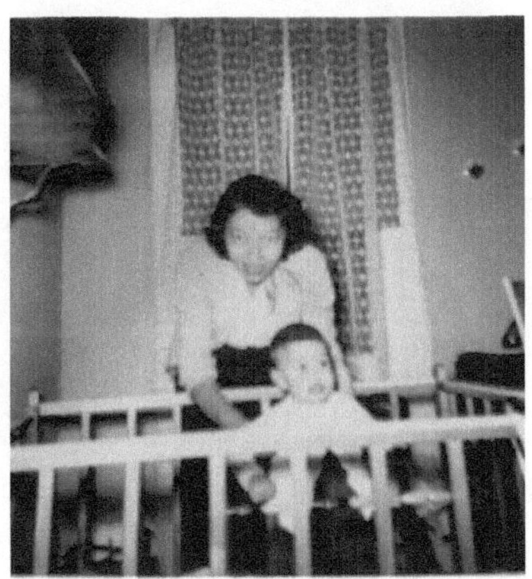

Mary & Rusell - 1955

Russ – 1955 Christmas

'Russell' 1st Birthday – 1955

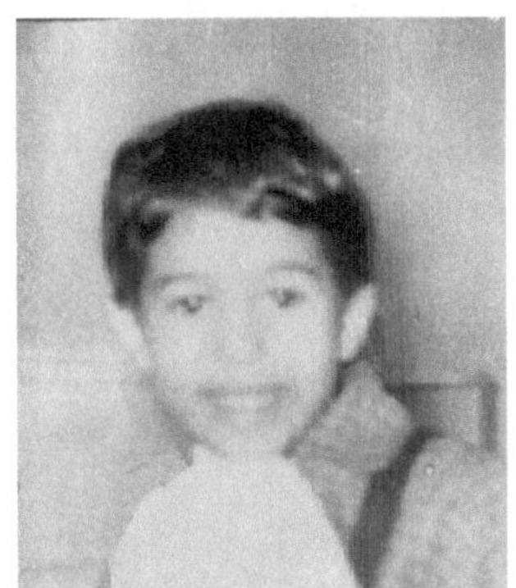

'Russell' – 1957   3 years old

'Russell & Mary' Fair St - 1955

' St. Patrick's Cathedral - New York

'Inside the church' – New York

Photo Credit – Paul Falardeau

' Life Hotel' formally 'Hotel Clinton'

Photo Credit- 20th Century Fox San Bernardino Sun

Pasco Franklin, Washington

Paul - 1970

Letter written to Mary from Paul

Jan 25, 1954

Dear Mary,

Received your letter this morning. I'm enclosing the $30.00 as promised. I wanted to explain some things to you over the phone, but so many people around the lobby—you know who, but it is not important. From what I understand the hotel has been sold and the new people are to come on the 1st of Feb, so I'll be out of a job here. I don't know what I am going to do after that as New York is very bad for jobs right now. I'll have to start looking soon. I do need a little rest as I am very nervous and losing a lot of weight. I only weigh 137 now and most of the food I eat won't stay down. I guess there's not much more for me to say at this time, but if ever I can do some thing—you know I will try. In the meantime, let me know if you get this as soon as possible as I don't know what's going to happen here.

Sincerely,

Paul

'Mary . A. Gonsalves' 1995

Russell .W. Gonsalves – 58 years old.

Chapter Eight

I was ready to return to the hotel with Paul as the clock struck past eight. However, he had a surprise in store—a carriage ride through Central Park. The idea was so unexpected that I was momentarily taken aback. I had already canceled on him once, and the thought of a leisurely carriage ride did sound appealing. After all, it meant I wouldn't have to walk.

Approaching the man sitting in front of the carriage, Paul told him we would like to ride. The gentleman introduced himself, "My name is Peter, like the Apostle, but more handsome." I laughed, finding humor in what the man said, Paul, but not so much. "And this beauty right here is Buttercup. I named her that cause she's sweet like one. She will glide you through the park's lush landscape with grace and poise as I tell you about the rich history dating back to the eighteen fifties."

Being the perfect gentleman, Paul helped me get up in the carriage, where a cozy blanket awaited me. "Are you Feeling a bit chilly, Mary? Let me cover you with this blanket," he said, draping it over my lap. I smiled at his kindness.

As we trotted along, I didn't know why this thought popped into my head, but I thought, I'm riding with Apostle Paul and Peter from the Bible; now, that's funny. I wanted to share my foolishness with Paul, but I thought it was best to keep it to myself.

During the ride, Peter informed us of many things, such as Central Park carriage rides, which have been going on since 1858. He also gave us the history of everything we saw, such as **Angels**

of the Waters (Bethesda Fountain), 1873, symbolizing clean water in New York. **Bust of Johann Christoph Friedrich von Schiller**, 1859, this was the first monument of Central Park. The German-American community donated it to honor the philosopher, poet, and playwright.

The Statue of Alexander Hamilton, built in 1880, commemorates one of the United States' Founding Fathers. The last two statues were of **Christopher Columbus** in 1894 and **William Shakespeare** in 1872. It was nice to learn the history of these famous people, who would be discussed forever. When Peter was done telling us about all the things we passed, he stayed silent so we could enjoy our time together.

Paul continued sharing things about his life, such as his first job at age ten, tending to the neighbor's yard, or when he chased his younger brother Harry off the porch so fast that he landed on his foot wrong, breaking his pinkie toe. With all the shared memories of his life back home in Montana, good and bad, I felt something was calling him back there, but I didn't know what. It was just a feeling I had in my gut.

Paul seemed restless with only a few more minutes left of the carriage ride. It was like this grown man was a toddler trying to sit still but couldn't. I couldn't figure out his problem until he handed me a small jewelry box with a blue ribbon tied around it. Now I understood. He was trying to pull it out of his inside jacket without being conspicuous. His hands were shaking, his eyes avoiding mine, his breath uneven. I didn't know how to react. I felt frozen in time, seeing his vulnerability laid bare before me. I couldn't help but feel a surge of empathy toward him.

"Mary, we've gotten to know each other over the past few weeks. And yes, I know you said you don't want a relationship, and I respect that. The box you're holding is just a symbol of what you mean to me. It's not much, but since you came into my life, you have made me want to be someone worth fighting for. Someone who wants to share every part of them with the other person. I can't explain it, but you, Mary, have healed my heart in ways I never knew possible," Paul declared with conviction.

My eyes widened in surprise, and my heart raced with mixed emotions. Paul's words touched me. I struggled to find the right words. I found myself in a profound dilemma. He was right. I had come to New York with the goal of self-discovery and personal growth, a journey that was becoming increasingly complex. Could I allow Paul to be more than just a friend? I craved companionship and had that with Paul, although without the romantic element. Yet, I couldn't deny the tumultuous feelings that stirred within me whenever I was with him. My mind was a battleground of conflicting emotions, and I was deeply engaged in this internal struggle.

I felt a smile spread across my face, like a schoolgirl who had just found her first crush. My heart raced as I looked into Paul's beautiful hazel eyes, and I mustered the courage to express my feelings without overstepping: "Paul, you didn't have to buy me anything. I understand your feeling for me and feel the same way, but…." I was torn between the joy of his affection and the fear of my expectations. It took all the courage I had to voice my inner turmoil.

My voice faltered, and Paul, ever patient and understanding, sensed my hesitation. He didn't rush me but gently encouraged me, "Go ahead, Mary. Open it." His reassuring gaze gave me the courage to continue.

I untied the blue ribbon from the box and lifted the cover. Inside was a breathtaking gold, diamond, and pearl double tulip brooch. The gold was a warm, rich hue; the diamonds sparkled like a constellation of stars, and the pearls were lustrous and perfectly round. This looked expensive, and I couldn't accept it. The gesture was nice, but what was he thinking? "Paul, I appreciate this beautiful gift, but I can't keep this."

He reached into the box, taking out the brooch. Unpinning the back, he leaned in carefully, pinning it to the right corner of my dress, and declared, "You can, Mary. I bought it because I wanted you to have something special. After all, you are someone special. I've met plenty of people in my line of work at the hotel, but I've never met someone as kind, funny, and beautiful as you are." Paul's voice, filled with profound sincerity and vulnerability, echoed in the evening air.

The carriage stopped before I could react to Paul's words. Peter helped me climb down, saying, "I hope you both had a wonderful time. Buttercup and I enjoyed showing you around Central Park." Nudging Paul with his elbow, I heard Peter tell Paul, "You're a lucky man."

Thankfully, a cab was conveniently parked across the street from the park, sparing us from needing to hail one. The clock was ticking toward ten, and I felt the full force of exhaustion. The soothing breeze from the carriage ride had done its job, and I knew that once I laid my head on my pillow, sleep would claim me instantly. It didn't take us long to return to the hotel, where Sergio greeted us, "Good evening to you both. I take it from the expressions on your faces that you've both had a wonderful time?"

Paul and I replied, "Yes," simultaneously, causing us both to express a hint of laughter. Sergio could see we were both tired, so he didn't keep us long—just enough to ask where we went for dinner and if I enjoyed the carriage ride through Central Park. Paul must have told him about the surprise he had planned for me seeing he asked about the carriage ride. Once we were in front of my hotel door, I took the opportunity to let Paul know how appreciative I was of the entire night, including the stunning brooch.

Our eyes locked, a silent plea for understanding. My heart raced between the desire to bridge the gap and the fear of shattering our friendship. Inside, a voice screamed, Ignore what you've said and kiss him! Paul took two steps toward me, but in a conflicting move, I stepped back, my heels hitting the door.

My knees trembled, and my palms were sweaty. Paul's smoldering smile, his arm over my shoulder against the hotel door, made me feel trapped but not scared. Our bodies were inches apart, and the thought of our lips touching made me tremble more. With his head on my left side and hand still on the door, Paul whispered, " Goodnight, Mary. May you have nothing but sweet dreams." Before walking away toward the elevator, he kissed me on the cheek, making it a bittersweet end to a beautiful night.

I didn't leave the hallway and go into my room until he was on the elevator. I watched as he and his incredibly desirable lips left. I was heartbroken, yet I couldn't blame him for not kissing me passionately on the lips. That was my own doing. I struggled with my boundaries, torn between what I desired and what I had decided. I forbade him to cross that line, explaining thatI only wanted a platonic friendship. I didn't want to think about it anymore, so I didn't. Instead, I got ready for bed and fell asleep.

Over the next couple of weeks, I worked on writing articles on topics ranging from women's dresses and men's suits to what every housewife cooked up for their man in the kitchen. When that became enough, I wrote about the hottest movie in theaters, but my all-time favorite piece had to be (this is me being sarcastic) how to remove bunions fast and effectively. That said, I was still grateful I was in a job I loved. I did, however, catch up with Isabella at Café Fanelli a week after my time with Paul. We had so much catching up to do that we drank several cups of coffee for over two hours. Her comforting presence and shared laughter made the time fly, and I cherished every moment.

She informed me about Mateo's improvement, mentioning that his Polio had improved significantly. However, due to weakness and dehydration, he still needed to take it easy over the next few months. Isabella also interrogated me about Paul until I broke. She was determined to know everything and wouldn't stop until I told her. I can honestly say Isabella is so loving and sweet, but she could make an onion cry. If the government ever needed someone to get information from our enemies, Isabella would be our best option. She has will and determination. Ultimately, she was happy I had someone to spend my days with.

My boss, Dean, called me this morning to share some exciting news. He's entrusting me with covering the story of Princess Elizabeth of York. On June 2, she would be crowned the Queen of seven independent Commonwealth countries. This is a significant event, and I'm eager to do my due diligence on the soon-to-be queen for an extraordinary story. But before I headed to the office, I planned to stop by Paul's room.

As I caught the elevator, I couldn't help but think about my plans with Paul tomorrow. I knew we had something scheduled, but I wanted to let him know that completing this critical article might affect the timing. Paul kindly offered to meet me at the office to walk me back to the hotel tonight. When I arrived at work, Dean was heading home for the day. He asked if I'd have the article done and leave it on his desk so he had it first thing in the morning. I told him that was my plan. I knew it was imperative to get it done sooner rather than later so that the editors, layout, and printing people had time to set it all up for Tuesday morning business.

Flipping the light on in my office, I got right to work. I slid a blank paper into my typewriter and began typing away. The headline would read,

"Princess Elizabeth Crowned Queen at Westminster Abbey."

Today marks an extraordinary day for the people of the United Kingdom. At the age of twenty-five, after Princess Elizabeth's father's death, King George the Sixth, she will be crowned queen. Her coronation, an initiation ceremony, occurs at Westminster Abbey in London. Here, she will take an oath, be anointed with holy oil, wear ceremonial jewelry, and be draped with robes. Her duties will include meetings with ambassadors, High Commissioners, newly appointed British ambassadors, and senior British and Commonwealth Armed Forces members.

The queen personally chooses events to attend daily, showing her empathy and understanding of her people's needs. These events may include school visits, military units, hospitals, and charities. She also holds private discussions with the Prime Minister once a week.

Princess Elizabeth's personal life is just as fascinating as her royal duties. She married Prince Philip on November 20, 1947, after meeting in 1934 at Princess Marina of Greece and Denmark's wedding to Prince George. The couple has two children, Charles the Third and Anne, born in 1948 and 1950, adding a personal touch to the royal family.

At the culmination of the procession, the majestic royal family will grace the balcony of Buckingham Palace, a sight to behold as they prepare to witness a grand flypast. In three awe-inspiring divisions, a hundred and sixty-eight jetfighters will soar overhead, each thirty seconds apart, in three divisions thirty seconds apart at a breathtaking height of fifteen hundred feet. The Coronation, a spectacle of regal magnificence, will be broadcast on the esteemed networks of CBS, NBC, DuMont, and ABC.

As I pulled the article out from the typewriter, I couldn't help but feel a surge of personal confidence in its quality. I knew it was a strong piece, but Dean had the final judgment. With unwavering assurance, I placed it on his desk and made my way to meet Paul outside in the front of the building.

The warm nighttime summer breeze, carrying the scent of blooming flowers and distant city lights, made walking back toward the hotel quite pleasant. Paul and I eagerly discussed our plans for the next day, each suggestion adding to our excitement. I have always been one to plan things out. I couldn't imagine just doing whatever whenever. It didn't make sense to me. Paul suggested we start by having breakfast at the diner up the street. From there, we could go to the Empire State Building and catch the ferry to the Statue of Liberty.

At this point, I was ready for anything as long as it was planned, and I had Paul by my side. We returned to the hotel just after nine, which gave me time to sink into the comfort of my bed, the soft glow of the TV adding to the relaxation. Only one show kept my interest long enough to fall asleep—the Red Button Show.

The following day, I was greeted by the sun peeking through the slight opening of the curtains, a gentle reminder that it was just before seven. With Paul and I planning to meet in the lobby by eight, I wasted no time and jumped in the shower. I consciously decided to push aside any worries about the article I wrote last night, knowing that if there were a problem, Dean would call the hotel and leave a message. I was determined to start the day with a fresh mind and all my attention on having a good time with Paul.

Last week, during a peaceful lunch break, I snuck out down the street to Bloomingdales, where I found a few summer dresses on sale. The red and white sheer dress I chose was not just a purchase but a promise of comfort. Its light fabric and comfortable fit, with sleeves that came down a quarter and the dress wrapping in the front just above my knees, made me feel at ease.I was delighted with my choice. For comfortable footwear, I chose my white ballet flats.

Anticipating the warm weather and the boat ride, I pinned up my hair to prevent frizz, leaving the rest to dance in the sea breeze. Before leaving, I adorned the right side of my dress, with the brooch Paul gave me last night and paired it with the small heart-shaped pearl earrings. As I finished with five minutes to spare, I couldn't help but feel the excitement building up. When the elevator doors opened, Paul stood leaning against the counter, talking to Sergio. I honestly believed my heart stopped for a second on how handsome he was. He didn't notice me immediately, which allowed me to marvel at the beautiful specimen of a man. Paul wore a solid navy blue polo shirt tucked into his white trousers and navy blue oxford shoes.

As I walked over, Sergio caught Pauls attention by pointing in my direction with a smile. It felt as if we were preparing for prom. Nervousness and excitement built. Paul initially turned his head, but when our eyes met, he turned his whole body toward me. We were now standing a foot apart. Paul's reaction was immediate, a gasp escaping his lips as he uttered, "Mary, every time you walk into a room, you take my breath away."

 Smiling, I replied, "Paul, you have a way of making me feel like I'm the only woman in the world." His eyes sparkled with admiration, and I could feel the warmth of his affection.

Reaching for both my hands, he declared in a single swoop, "Mary, you're the only woman I see standing here that could stop a thousand beating hearts at a drop of a dime." His words were a passionate declaration, filling the air with intensity and romance.

Paul had a way with words, and I found myself hanging on to every one of them. His charm was undeniable, making me feel safe with him. Even when he let go of one hand, he held the other as we walked out of the hotel. Months ago, I would have never allowed this level of intimacy. He had a pull on me, like a moth to a flame, and I found myself drawn to him despite my initial reservations.

Paul and I had breakfast at Old John's Diner, a place with a delightful atmosphere. The black and white checkered floors caught my eye when I stepped in, gleaming with a beautiful Polish shine. We chose to sit in one of the cream leather booths, away from the high stools at the bar. I ordered a cup of tea, a perfectly scrambled dry egg, and a slice of wheat toast while Paul had his usual black coffee and a plate of French toast with crispy bacon. The breakfast was so delicious it left us craving for more.

We decided to walk to the Empire State Building because the temperature was only seventy-five degrees, which was not too hot. Along the way, we stopped at a few stores to look around. One of the stores was a quaint little bookshop where I found some engaging titles. Another was a souvenir shop filled with trinkets and memorabilia. A few things caught my eye, but I did not buy anything because I didn't want to carry it around all day while we were out. We chose to go all the way to the top of the Empire State Building, which was one hundred and two floors. Once up there, Paul slid two quarters into the binoculars so I could get a closer look at the city.

Pairing through the binoculars, I was greeted with a site that filled me with awe. The beauty of Central Park, the grandeur of the World Trade Center, the vibrant billboards of Times Square, the majesty of the Chrysler building, and the iconic Statue of Liberty all laid out before me in a breathtaking panorama. We strolled around the observation deck, soaking in the views from every angle. As we prepared to leave, the anticipation of the ferry ride to the Statue of Liberty filled us with excitement. Paul hailed a cab to take us to Battery Park, where our next adventure awaited.

As we arrived, an energetic crowd was already gathered, eagerly anticipating the ferry's departure. Paul, with his usual charm, approached the ticketing gentleman, and after the exchange fare, we secured a seat toward the front of the ferry. The vessel quickly filled with a lively crowd, all eager for the journey ahead. The ferry was set to depart at noon, and it was eleven-fifty. Paul could see the eagerness in my eyes.

He sat beside me, his hand reaching for mine, as he said, " I'm truly enjoying this, Mary. I hope you are, too." His words echoed my feelings, and I couldn't help but smile in agreement.

He knew I was, yet I replied, "I am, Paul. Thank you for spending the day with me."

"There's no one I'd rather spend time with than you, Mary," he confessed, his voice filled with nervousness and sincerity as his eyes locked with mine.

As the clock struck noon, the ferry captain's voice cut through the air, " We are about to embark on a journey. The ride is approximately fifteen minutes. Get ready to be captivated by the sights along the way. Thank you." The anticipation of adventure filled the air.

The fresh sea breeze spellbound Paul and me as we neared the island. The breathtaking view of the Brooklyn Bridge and the surrounding natural beauty, with the iconic New York City skyline stretching across the Hudson, left us in absolute awe. After disembarking, we began our ascent of one hundred ninety-two steps to reach the pedestal viewing deck. The view was beyond our wildest dreams-crystal clear skies and the iconic New York City skyline stretching across the Hudson. We wandered around, our hearts filled with appreciation for the stunning masterpiece of nature and architecture.

The time had flown by, and we found ourselves having to return to the ferry. We enjoyed each other's company and laughter, which created a remarkable friendship between us both. Paul and I chose to sit in the back, this time to watch as Lady Liberty disappeared from our view. When we docked, it was around three-thirty, and I was pretty thirsty and hungry, so Paul suggested we could either find a place now or wait until we got closer to the hotel. I figured what was a little longer, so we jumped back in a cab and headed back.

As we continued toward the hotel, I stopped to grab a hot dog at a vendor on 5th Ave to hold me over until dinner. Because Paul wanted to take me out tonight, I suggested we part ways for a while so I could rest and freshen up before our evening plans. He hinted at a surprise location—a place with a breathtaking view of the city. I agreed as he asked, " Would it be fine if I swing by your room to pick you up at seven-thirty?"

"Yes, that would be fine, Paul," I replied, giddy and excited for the evening ahead.

As I stopped by the front desk to check for messages, Sergio informed me that Dean and my mother had both called. The fact that my mother was calling a day earlier than our usual Sunday catch-up immediately caught my attention. Panic set in as I sensed something was amiss. I hurried over to the phone across the way in the lobby. Dialing home, it rang several times before my mother answered the phone, "Hello." Her voice sounded as normal as any other time I called to speak to her, but her unexpected nature intrigued me.

"Mother, It's me. I'm worried about you. Are you okay? Do you need me to come home?" I asked, my concern evident in my voice.

"Mary, I should be asking you if you're okay. Why do you think I'm not okay or need you to come home? Can't a mother surprise her daughter with a phone call without something wrong?"

"Of course, but we always talked on Sunday, so when you called today, I thought...I was surprised and a bit worried. It's not like you to call on a Saturday, making me wonder if something was wrong."

"I promise, dear, nothing is wrong. I just wanted to see how you've been. Anything new you'd like to share?" She asked in a hinting kind of way.

"Well, Dean this week gave me the front page again. He asked me to write a piece on Princess Elizabeth becoming Queen this Tuesday. I just got back to the hotel, and he also called. Part of me is worried now. He doesn't usually call unless he's changing my schedule on what I'm supposed to write for the week, which he has done a few times."

"I'm sure it's nothing, Mary. It would help if you stopped second-guessing your work. You're wonderful at what you do. So where were you, if I may ask?"

"I went out early this morning for breakfast, then headed to the Empire State Building before taking a ferry ride to the Statue of Liberty. It was fascinating, and I enjoyed myself."

"So you went out by yourself for the day? She asked in an innocent tone, trying not to overstep.

It's been several months and many phone calls later, and I've yet to tell her about Paul. I wasn't sure I wanted to or what she would say. He's a significant part of my life now, and I'm unsure how to bring it up.

"Mary, are you still there, "she called out.

"Yes, I'm still here, and to answer your question, no. I didn't go by myself. I will tell you about him, but you must promise not to make a big deal. Promise?" I asked, hoping she would respect my wishes.

I could hear her take a deep breath before she answered, "Yes, I promise."

"His name is Paul. I met him the first day I came to New York. He works for the hotel where I'm staying. He's very handsome and kind. But before you let your mind wander thinking that we are more than friends, we are not. I've informed him that I'm here to establish myself in the writing world of journalism." I expressed not wanting to go any further.

"May I ask you just one thing, and I'll leave it alone?"

"Yes, that's fine, go ahead."

"Do you ever think you'll make time for love in your life, honey?"

Her question pierced me like a dagger. I know she yearns for me to find love and share that longing, but I dread that I will lose sight of my goals if I allow myself to love. I shared my vulnerability with her about Paul, hoping she would empathize with my struggle.

"I was determined to keep my distance when I first met Paul. Now, I cannot shake the thought of him, which terrifies me. He's everything I never thought I wanted—yet he's everything I want. What do I do?" I asked my mother, knowing she knew what loving another felt like.

"Mary, Love is taking risks. If we live life always afraid of the what-ifs, then we exist in this world without purpose. You can work your whole life striving to be known, but at the end of the day, what good is it if you have no one to share it with? My marriage to your father might not have been picture-perfect, but at least I got to experience what it was to love someone, even if his love looked different. Yes, I didn't get to live out my days with my prince charming, but I have my happily ever after. **You!**"

My mother always knew exactly what to say and when to say it. I wiped the tears that fell down the sides of my face and said, "I do miss you, Mom. Thanks for that."

"You are my life, Mary, and someday, when you have a child of your own, you'll know exactly what to say to them that will shape their life and give them the courage to live fearlessly. That's all I want for you is to live fearlessly." We stayed on the phone for a few more minutes before I reminded my mother that I still needed to call my boss. I assured her that I would call next week before hanging up.

I called Dean back, and he answered after one ring, "Hello."

"Hi, Dean. It's Mary; I'm returning your call. I hope I'm not disturbing you.

"Hello, Mary. I won't take up too much of your time. I just wanted to call to let you know your article is great. We will be running it on Tuesday. I couldn't be happier with your work. Go out and celebrate. You deserve it, and I'll see you Monday."

"Thank you, Dean. I'm glad you thought it was great, and yes, I will be going out to celebrate this evening. Have a wonderful rest of your weekend. See you Monday."

With Dean's approval of my work, I could finally look forward to a relaxing evening with Paul, free from any work-related distractions. I had enough time for a quick nap before preparing for the night. Before I rested, I carefully selected my outfit, ensuring I wouldn't be rushed at the last minute. I was determined to follow my mother's advice and embrace the moment. Live freely.

I called Sergio, "Front desk, Sergio speaking. How may I assist you?"

"Hello, Sergio, this is Mary. Would you be so kind as to ring my room in half an hour, please?"

"Certainly, Miss Mary. Is there anything else I can assist you with?" He asked in that kind, sweet voice as always.

"No. That will be it. I appreciate your assistance, Sergio. Thank you."

After hanging up, I decided to slide off my shoes and lay on the bed, not bothering to change, as I would get up in a bit to get ready. As usual, I turned on the TV to drown out the city noise, making it easier to fall fast asleep.

Chapter Ten

The time had come. Paul would knock on my door any minute, and I was more nervous than ever. In my conversation with my mother earlier in the day, it kept replaying in my mind: Live fearlessly, and so I was determined to do just that tonight. I pulled out my best dress, a stunning piece I had spotted at Bergdorf Goodman a few weeks back. I couldn't stop staring at it through the showroom window. I felt it was made for me, so I walked straight in, told the woman my size, and took it.

It was out of my price range, but I didn't care. I wanted to buy something at least once in my lifetime without worrying about the cost. Honestly, though, I thought about taking it back. Every time I thought about the price I paid, I wanted to throw up a little, but I pushed through and kept it. Now that I have it on, I feel a transformation from nervousness to fearlessness and beauty. The sheer pink and white Organza lace cocktail dress fit perfectly, and it's as if it had given me a newfound sense of empowerment.

I've paired it with my three-inch white heels, and for jewelry, I've chosen the single white pearl necklace that my grandmother bought me last year. I curled my soft brown shoulder-length hair just enough to give it some bounce. Since tonight's temperature wouldn't be too bad, I chose not to pin any of it up. The only make-up I applied was my light pink lipstick and blush, allowing both to accent my lips and cheekbones. As I put my compact mirror into my purse, I heard a knock on the door. "Come in," I said.

The door opened, and Paul walked in smiling while holding a bouquet of long-stem yellow roses in a vase. I swallowed so hard that it echoed in the back of my ears. He was dressed like he had just done a photoshoot for GQ. You know those magazines women buy to dream of what they wish their husbands looked like? I felt a surge of confidence and excitement as I took in his appearance, starkly contrasting my earlier nervousness. He was wearing a gray three-piece suit with a white colored shirt and black shoes that looked to be recently shined. The scent of his cologne filled the air, adding to the anticipation.

Every feeling in my body roared with excitement. He took a few steps closer to hand me the flowers and said," These are for you. I hope you like them. I took a chance with roses. I chose yellow because it reminded me of how intense and beautiful you are. Every time we get together, it's like seeing you for the first time. I can still remember that day like it was yesterday.I thought, my God, am I dreaming?" His words were so intense that it was as if he was reliving that moment again.

Every word he spoke felt like it was rehearsed as if he was playing the part of Laurance Olivier or Humphrey Bogart in a romantic film, but I didn't care. I longed to love and be loved. I yearned for someone to see me, and he did. I knew he cared for me, but I didn't know if he felt the same as me. All the feelings I continuously tried to suppress came rushing in. I couldn't take it anymore. I was deeply, madly in love with Paul, and his actions made it harder to deny.

"Thank you, Paul. These are stunning," I said as I placed them on my nightstand., feeling deeply appreciative of his romantic gesture.

"Beautiful flowers for a beautiful lady," he declared, being as charming as always. His charm, like a spell, always managed to captivate me, leaving me feeling both flattered and apprehensive. I couldn't help but wonder if it was just a façade or if he genuinely had the same feelings for me. Either way, I loved him, and that terrified me.

"Shall we go? I'm famished." I asked as my stomach started to growl. I was eager to enjoy the evening before sounds started to embarrass me again, as they had done before. I grabbed the light shawl I had laid on the bed before we headed out the door. Paul and I ate at a place called Gallagher's Steakhouse. The aroma of sizzling steaks filled the air, and the soft glow of the candle on our table added to the romantic ambiance.

We both had prime rib, mashed potatoes, and steamed broccoli. When we finished, Paul asked if I would like to listen to jazz at Birdland. I thought it would be fun since I had never been to a jazz club, so we headed to three Fifteen West Forty-fourth St.

The place was named after the legendary jazz musician Charlie "Bird" Parker. We were led to a small table close to the stage when we entered. Every other table was round or square, lined with white tablecloths and a small lit candle in the center. The room was filled with smoke, and red lighting pointed to the stage. Pictures of legendary people from past and present who had performed at the Birdland were hung on the walls. The person who graced us with his musical talents was Dizzy Gillespie. I wasn't too familiar with him, yet I heard of him.

Each musician's performance left a profound impact. Dizzy Gillespie's trumpet playing was unlike anything I had ever heard before. The extraordinary gifts of Charlie David and Miles Davis further enriched the evening. Their performances inspired me deeply, and I felt privileged to be in their audience.

Paul and I strolled back to the hotel as the night drew closer. The moonlight cast a serene glow, and I could see the reflection of his beautiful eyes. We didn't exchange many words, but he reached for my hand, and I accepted. Our fingers intertwined, yet I felt a distance. I longed to bridge that gap, to express my feelings for him. I yearned for that moment.

"Mary, what are you thinking about?" He asked as if he knew my mind was going full speed ahead.

"Just life. That's all, " I answered as casually as I could without drawing attention.

He squeezed my hand a little tighter and replied, "Just life. Huh. Is this life you're thinking about now or in the future?"

"Both, " I answered as I looked down while we continued walking.

Before Paul could further question me, we arrived back at the hotel. As we stood at the elevator waiting for it to arrive, he asked, " I don't want to upset you, Mary, but I was wondering if you'd like to join me in my room for a nightcap?"

My mother's voice played in my head again: Live fearlessly. If I thought about the question too long, I'd chicken out, so I replied, "Sure, I'd like that." A moment later, the elevator chimed, and the doors opened. Still holding my hand, we step in together. I kept telling myself to breathe and that I was going for a nightcap, nothing more. Once we arrived at Paul's room, he told me to get comfortable. I could sit on his bed or grab the chair near his writing desk. I chose the chair.

However, I did pull it next to the bed where I assumed he would sit, seeing those were the only two options for either of us. Paul walked over toward the window, where he drew the curtains closed. I felt my mouth become dry and my hands become clammy. I asked if I could use his bathroom.

He pointed over to the door on the left and asked, "Are you okay?"

Walking toward the bathroom, I fought to keep my voice steady as I replied, "Yes. I'm good. Thanks."

When I returned, Paul asked, "What would you like?"

I knew what he was asking, yet I wanted to say, I'd like you to tell me you love me. That life without me isn't worth living. I'd like you to say we will get married and have babies, but instead, I said, "Whatever you're having is fine."

Paul poured me a whisky, something I'd never drank and never will again. I didn't want to waste it or insult him, so I took small sips until it was gone. It didn't take him long to finish his first glass before he poured himself another. I didn't say much, and neither did he. I felt he was as nervous as I was. Finally, he popped off the bed and asked, "Music, you like music?"

At first, I wasn't sure if he was asking or telling me. I figured I'd clarify the matter: "I do like music. I wasn't sure if you were asking or telling me. Either way, I bet you can guess by the jazz we heard tonight, " I replied, being a little playful.

"Okay, okay, that was sort of my fault. It's just I'm nervous if you can't tell. I don't know why, either. We spend all our free time together. Let me turn on the radio. Maybe I can find something we will enjoy listening to."

Paul changed the station until he found Frank Sinatra's song, **All The Things You Are**. Walking over to me, he asked, "May I have this dance?"

I stood up and reached out for his hand. He pulled me close to his body, and we began to sway back and forth as he hummed softly to the song. I laid my head on his shoulder, thinking there was no other place I'd rather be than in his arms. When the song was over, we continued to dance to several more, neither of us wanting to let go of each other's embrace. It wasn't until Paul started singing, **With These Hands**, by **Eddie Fisher,** one of my favorites, that I realized I was falling in love with him more and more. I couldn't deny it. When a man sings, with these hands, I'll cling to you forever and a day, he must feel the same.

I lifted my head off his shoulder and pulled back just enough to face each other, wanting to kiss him. My mind was racing with excitement and fear, but my heart was sure. He then repositioned his hands. His left held the small of my back while his right cradled the back of my head before his lips met mine. It was nice. I always thought people exaggerated when they said, kissing him or her was like fireworks, or I felt like we were floating, yet that's precisely how I felt. The intensity of that moment was overwhelming, a feeling I can't quite put into words.

Our bodies were entangled with passion. This was the first time I had thrown caution to the wind. I did not have a care in the world. For the first time in my life, I let myself be free. It was a moment of personal growth, a step toward understanding my desires and needs. I could get into more details, but I'm sure you know what happened next.

I rolled over the following day, expecting to find Paul beside me, but he wasn't there. Where was he? Was he regretting last night? Worried he felt like he made a mistake, I quickly grabbed my clothes and dressed. Reaching for my shoes, I noticed the left one went missing. It must've been under the bed, I thought. Getting on all fours, I slid my head under to see if I could find it when I heard Paul ask, "Mary, what are you doing? Please tell me you didn't think I was hiding from you under there?"

Slowly sliding back from under the bed after finding my shoe, I heard Paul laughing. His attempt to hide his smile was so endearing it made me chuckle. He reached for my hand to help me up. I sat on the bed, sliding on my other shoe while smirking. He tried not to smile, but he did, which made me smile back. We both laughed.

"Where did you go?" I asked.

"Why did you miss me?" he asked, wondering and waiting for my reply.

"Sure, I guess," I answered, teasing him.

"Mary, I did want to talk to you about something, " he said, sounding slightly serious.

"Can it wait? I have a few things I need to get done today. Maybe we can catch up later," I asked, hoping he would agree.

"Yeah, that's fine. We can catch up later."

I grabbed my purse, kissed him goodbye, and headed for my room. First, I took a quick shower, changed, and headed to the corner deli to grab a sandwich, chips, and a few Cokes for later. It was Sunday, and I eagerly looked forward to sharing with my mother how the night went with Paul, minus the romance. Also, I needed to unwind and catch up on some articles for the newspaper this week.

Before heading back to my room to relax, I called my mother. We talked for a few minutes as she was doing laundry and cleaning the house. She was excited to hear that I had a good time with Paul. I also shared with her that I was falling in love with him. I did, however, tell her that I hadn't said those three words to him just yet. She informed me that those words come naturally when you least expect them.

I asked how everything was back home. She informed me that Mrs. McIntyre, our neighbor, brought a dog home for her kids, but it barks all night. Being the kind-hearted woman that my mother is, she has chosen to sleep with earplugs in her ears at night to avoid confrontation. I tried not to laugh, as I was sure she wouldn't appreciate it. I told her how much I missed her and that I would call again next Sunday before ending the call.

For the next several hours, I tried writing new things for the newspaper, but I could only think of Paul and the night we shared. As much as I loved spending time with him, I had to remind myself not to forget my primary purpose: my career. Concentrating was a struggle, and I eventually gave up on any writing as it was later in the afternoon. Instead, I turned on the TV and watched three hours of back-to-back I Love Lucy while eating dinner on my bed.

As the night went on, I got ready for bed. I thought about stopping by Paul's room, but I felt like I needed time to digest all that had transpired the night before. Crawling under the cover, I continued to watch TV until I dozed off.

Chapter Eleven

It's the first week of September, and I've been in New York for six months. My job has been going well. Dean just gave me another story to be featured on the front page, plus a raise, but the real highlight of these past months has been my time with Paul. We've been inseparable, and just last week, we declared our love for each other. I couldn't be happier.

Paul and I have been eagerly anticipating our trip to Bill Miller's Riviera in Fort Lee, New Jersey, to see Frank Sinatra perform. I was incredibly excited about seeing Ole Blue Eyes live. However, the need to focus on work was paramount amidst the excitement. Paul and I have been working nonstop, and right now, I need to get to the office to write up my next article. With Dean on vacation, I must ensure this article is front-page worthy. The story I'm about to write slightly differs from what I'm used to writing, but it's a task I'm fully committed to. It's a book turned into a movie about to be released in just a few days.

I wanted to ensure that I knew exactly what I was writing about, so I stopped at the local bookstore and bought the book to read. My job was to inform people. I couldn't tell them to see this movie if I had no idea what it was about or if it was good. However, I was willing to watch the film just because Frank Sinatra was starring in it, and I enjoyed Frank.

While waiting for the elevator, I was lost in my thoughts when I heard Paul call my name as he walked my way. His unexpected presence brought a smile to my face. "Mary, where do you think you're sneaking off to?" he asked, taking my hand to twirl me around before pressing his lips against mine.

The elevator doors opened, and I jumped in quickly. As they closed, I couldn't help but express my love: "I'll be back before you know it. I love you." The words lingered in the air, filled with warmth and affection.

Even though the doors were closed, I could hear Paul yell, "Love you too, Mary."

When I arrived at work, I headed to my office, where I laid the book and my notes on the side of my desk. Once again, starting with a blank sheet of paper in the typewriter, I pondered the headline's title.

"From Here To Eternity"

Prepare to be captivated by this extraordinary film, starring Burt Lancaster, Montgomery Clift, Deborah Kerr, Donna Reed, and the legendary Frank Sinatra. Set in 1941, this film is a compelling narrative that promises to satisfy you deeply. It follows the emotional journey of three United States Army soldiers stationed in Hawaii, leading up to the pivotal event of the Pearl Harbor attack, a tragic accident, a forbidden romance, and the unyielding war that will change the course of their lives. This film is a powerful reminder of the impact of true bravery, taking risks, and determination in the face of uncertainty.

This film is a must-see based on James Jones's book. While some argue that the book is always superior to the movie, the only way to truly understand is to purchase a ticket and experience this emotional rollercoaster. Check local listing for showtimes.

When I was done and satisfied, I laid it on Margaret's desk. Dean would still be on vacation when the article needed to be printed, so she would ensure it was all set before printing. Grabbing my notes and purse, I shut off the office light and headed out. I usually walked back to the hotel with Paul as it was safer, but I could not find him. A sense of concern for his safety crept in, seeing that he was not like him.

The sky was ominously dark, threatening to unleash a downpour at any moment. I urgently flagged down a cab that had just whizzed past. Sensing the urgency, the driver slammed his brakes, threw the car into reverse, and stopped. He leaped out and opened the door, urging me to hurry. Without a second thought, I was in the cab, ready to go.

Seven minutes later, we arrived at the hotel. I paid the driver and hurried into the lobby, my eyes scanning the room period there, across the room, was Paul, engrossed in a heated phone conversation. His body language was tense, and his usual calm demeanor was replaced by visible distress. It was a sight I had never seen before, leaving me uneasy. I casually approached the front desk to avoid him noticing me, "Sergio, could you direct me to the stairs? I need to go up to my room." I asked, trying to maintain an air of nonchalance.

"Is everything okay, Mary? The elevators work, you know." Sergio asked with a confused look on his face.

"Yes, everything Is fine," I replied, hoping he would point me in the right direction.

Pointing, Sergio said, "Just go down the hall, and you'll see a door that reads: Emergency stairs. He asked again if I was okay, and I gave him the same answer before leaving for my room.

After changing into comfortable clothes, I wanted to reach out to Paul, but I respected his need for space. As I lay on the bed, I found it difficult to shake off the worry about what might be troubling him. The only person he ever mentioned was his family. Maybe he was upset with one of them. I tried to push the thought aside and relax, but his distress had unsettled me. Hours later, I felt a wave of nausea. It was as if my body was mirroring the unease I felt about

Paul's situation. I tried to eat, but nothing stayed down. I attributed it to my concern for Paul and decided to rest.

The next day, I crossed paths with Paul as he helped a guest with their luggage. We didn't have much time to talk, but we had planned to meet later at The Russian Tea Room. While waiting for his shift to end, I explored the city and shopped for myself. My first stop was Barnes and Noble, of course. After finishing up the book I borrowed from the library and returning it, I decided I might buy one today.

I walked around trying to find a good mystery to read. I considered buying and reading another Agatha Christie book or Erle Stanley Gardner—both authors I enjoyed equally. I own over twenty books from Christie's collection but only a handful of Garner's. I walked around a bit longer, looking at the newest fashion magazines that hit the stand yesterday before making my choice. I decided to buy both the newest Christie and Garner books, seeing that they both sounded intriguing.

After leaving the bookstore, I found myself in Macy's, where I thought about buying my mother a nice blouse or a knickknack. As I browsed through the racks, I couldn't help but think about how my mother's face would light up if I sent her a gift she wasn't expecting. I couldn't find anything on the racks that my mother would possibly wear, so I scratched that idea. There were many little knickknacks, but nothing jumped out at me either.

It wasn't until I passed by a table of beautiful, bold, sheer scarves that I knew this would be a great gift. She would wear it even if it weren't her favorite color. She just loved scarves. I took it to the checkout counter, where a young girl with a bright smile asked if it was a gift or for myself. I informed her that I was purchasing it for my mother, who was back in Massachusetts. She offered to gift wrap it for no extra charge, a gesture that warmed my heart. I kindly accepted her offer.

As I continued my day, I stood before the majestic Saint Patrick's Cathedral. I remembered Sister Mary's offer of spiritual guidance and decided to seek her out. A wave of relief washed over me as I stepped into the church. I spotted Sister Mary and patiently waited for her to finish her conversation with a young couple. Her familiar smile and warm greeting instantly put me at ease, comforting me in a way only spiritual guidance could.

"Mary, it's so good to see you again. Ever since our paths crossed, I've thought about you. Come, sit, let's catch up," she said.

I followed her into the back part of the church where her office was. I asked her if I was taking her away from her important work, serving the Lord. She laughed and replied, as she reached for my hand, "Mary, I never stop doing the Lord's work. You, my dear, are one of God's children. Together, fellowshipping about life is doing God's work. So tell me, what's been going on with you? Are you doing well?"

"I am, or though I thought I was. I feel burdened by something, yet I'm not sure what that something is. Does that even make sense?" I asked.

"Yes, my dear. Believe it or not, many people feel burdened by something they have yet experienced. It's there; we choose to suppress it rather than face it head-on, fearing that we can not handle it. I can give you the best advice, or I can give you what you want to hear. You have to be willing to apply what I give you so that you can come out of it on the other side. Which would you like?" She asked with such conviction.

Of course, I wanted the best advice. If anyone could help me, it was Sister Mary. I trusted her wisdom and experience and answered, "That's an easy choice. I chose you to give it to me straight."

"Oh, Mary, my child, you have to understand. The advice I'm about to give you comes from God through me. He's the only person who can help, heal, and save, but I can give it to you straight. What you do with it is up to you. Remember, God is always with you on this journey. Everything you see in me is grace from God. It's a gift.

Ask the Lord to reveal what's causing this heavy burden; pray for peace and understanding. He will show you, but in his time, when He knows you can handle it. You have to be patient," she said with truth.

I wanted her to shoot it to me straight, and she did. I felt she wanted me to reach deep down and tell her exactly what was happening, or maybe that was just my overwhelming guilt. Either way, something was stirring my soul, and I felt I needed to confess to figure out where my life was supposed to go next.

"Sister Mary, Can I be honest? I'm unsure if this is what's been burdening me, but I can't think of anything else, so I must discuss it. Is that alright? Do you have time?"

"I have as much time as you need, Mary," she replied with a smile that comforted me and made me feel safe.

"Okay, so when we first met, I shared with you how I was focused on my career, trying to make a name for myself in journalism, and I have done that. I was hired at the New York Herald Tribune, and it's going great. My boss, Dean, has challenged me, and I've grown. I am grateful for that. I've met a few people along the way who have become friends, particularly this young lady named Isabella, who I met here months ago."

"Yes, Isabella and her son, sweet Mataeo." She said.

"You know them," I asked, realizing right then what a stupid question that was. Of course, Sister Mary would know them; Isabella said she comes here every day to pray.

Sister Mary replied, "Isabella and her entire family had been coming here for years, but as you know, over time, she lost both her parents and came close to losing Mateo. She has been through some dark times, yet through it all, she's remained faithful to God. I am not saying she hasn't questioned Him, but her faith has gotten her to the other side. I'm sorry, we are getting off-topic; please continue with what you were saying, Mary."

I continued, "So, over the past several months, I've been somewhat involved with someone who works at the hotel where I'm staying. When I first met him, I explained that I didn't need any distractions and was here in New York to pursue my career, but something happened."

"I know what happened, Mary. You fell in love with him, and that's okay. We all want to be loved by someone, but we must remember that the love we seek may not always be reciprocated as we want it to be. You must be honest if you're unsure about where this is going. Did he hurt you?" She asked in a concerned tone.

"No. Not at all, but he's keeping something from me. I can feel it, but in his defense, he did want to talk to me about something a while back, but I was busy and haven't thought about it until now."

"Well, let me leave you with this: You can cry in the storm or dance in the rain. If you ignore what he needs to tell you because you fear it will break your heart, you'll never find happiness, but if you choose to listen to what he needs to tell you, it might just work out the way you want it to."

Sister Mary, whom I now consider a friend and confidant, offered some hard truths and insightful advice. After sitting with her for a while, I thanked her for listening and being someone I could talk to. Before leaving, she asked if I minded if she prayed for me, and of course, I was okay with it. I knew I could use some prayers right about now in my situation.

It was past four, and Paul's shift was ending. We had plans, and I knew he'd be wondering where I was, so I hurried back to the hotel. I thought I'd catch him in the lobby before I went to my room to get ready, but I didn't. I stopped by the desk to ask if there were any messages for me, and there wasn't, and I was grateful. I didn't need any distractions tonight. I wanted Paul and I to be able to talk.

As I got ready, I started to feel sick again. I couldn't understand what was going on. It was coming in waves. Maybe it was all the running around I was doing or not eating three meals a day like the average person. Whatever it was, I wouldn't let it keep me from spending time with Paul and going to the Russian Tea Room.

I heard a knock on the door and hollered, "Come in. I'm almost done getting ready."

I sprayed a little perfume in the air and walked directly in its path. My mother told me that's how you get the right amount on you without choking out everyone in a room. Putting on my jewelry was the last thing I needed. I slid my gold bangle bracelet on my right wrist and a Teardrop necklace around my neck to complete my attire. Walking out of the bathroom, there stood Paul, smiling. I somehow felt nervous being in his presence. He walked over and kissed me, and although I thought he would compliment me like he always did, he asked, "Are you ready?"

It was then I knew something was wrong, but I didn't ask, I just replied, "Yes,"

Chapter Twelve

Arriving at the Russian tea room at 6:00, I was excited. Thanks to Paul's reservations, we were promptly seated, avoiding the usual wait. This place never seemed to slow down, a favorite haunt of many celebrities. I couldn't help but hope to spot one. It didn't matter who, just the thrill of seeing a celebrity. Our table, strategically placed near the entrance, added to the excitement.

The décor in the restaurant was exquisite. The room was adorned with gold and red, booths lined across the back wall, and several square tables with chairs strategically placed in the middle. The walls were decorated with intricate Russian motifs and pictures of celebrities who frequented the place. There was a wall that separated the dining room from the bar, where people came to relax with a drink if they chose not to eat. Our waiter was dressed in a distinctive uniform: a double-breasted black coat with a tail and gold buttons lined his jacket. Underneath his coat was a collared, long white shirt as the sleeve of the cuffs poked out from his coat.

Our waiter, a tall man with a thin mustache, was very polite and recited tonight's specials. I ordered Chicken Kyiv, a breaded chicken breast stuffed with butter and herbs, with creamy mashed potato, while Paul had Pelmeni, Russian dumplings filled with meat served in a rich broth with freshly baked rolls. While we waited for our meals, Paul started a conversation that surprised me. After all, he had been pretty quiet since we met up.

"So, Mary, did you have a good day?" he asked.

"I did. I went shopping at a couple of stores. I bought myself two books and then found a nice scarf for my mother that I thought she would like before running into a friend. We talked for a while, and then I headed back to meet up with you."

"What about you? How was work today?" I asked, even though I knew he would say the same thing as always.

"It was work. People never see me as a person doing a job. They see me as a bellhop who they think will never amount to anything except that, a bellhop," He replied sarcastically.

Okay, so that wasn't Paul's usual response. I was wrong, and now there was no way I would have the "talk" with him tonight. The talk was something I had been avoiding for a while: a conversation about our relationship and where it was heading. I felt uncomfortable and wanted to leave but stayed, knowing the food was coming. I sipped my Earl tea while Paul polished off his gin and tonic.

As the waiter arrived with our food, Paul promptly ordered another drink. I struggled to contain my emotions, disappointed and frustrated at his behavior. The passing time did little to ease the tension, and I found it difficult to eat, my stomach still churning from the earlier incident. In stark contrast, Paul seemed more interested in his drinks than his food. He was on his fourth before I suggested we return to the hotel.

I knew it was time to leave when Paul spoke to me loudly and rudely, asking, "What's your problem, Mary? Are you not having a good time? I mean, come on. All I do is wine and dine you. Am I not enough for you anymore?"

Despite the embarrassment, I found the strength to stand up, leave some money on the table, and walk out of the restaurant, leaving Paul behind. I took a cab back to the hotel, where I tossed and turned all night. I couldn't believe how I was treated. I felt broken. After crying for what seemed like an eternity, I knew my only choice was to walk away. I loved Paul, but I didn't want to see him anymore. My priority shifted after Paul's ridiculous outburst at the restaurant, but my determination to succeed remained.

As days passed, I avoided Paul like the plague. I requested that Sergio not let him on my floor unless he was assisting other guests. He kindly obliged without prying into the details. This experience, though painful, only made me stronger. Even with the turmoil in my personal life, I was determined not to let it affect my professional life. I continued to work hard for Dean, putting out story after story.

I called my mother and confided in her what had transpired between Paul and me. She could hear how broken up I was over the entire thing and assured me I would come out of it on the other side. She reminded me of my worth when she said, "Remember, Mary, you should never have to explain to someone how you deserve to be loved. Your worth should always be recognized without question, my dear sweet daughter." I couldn't hold back the tears. She was right. I needed to hear just that. From that day, I pushed forward, looking toward my future.

Days turned into weeks, and weeks turned into another month. I was taking care of myself, yet the day came when I needed to talk to Paul. I asked Sergio to leave a message at the desk to ensure he got it when he finished work. As always, he agreed to my request. The note I wrote to Paul was direct. It read: *Paul, I need to speak to you tonight. I will meet you in the lobby at six o'clock sharp. Please be there, Mary.*

Paul and I had planned a night at Bill Miller's Riviera a few months back, which coincidentally was tonight. If he still wanted to go, I'd go because what I had to say was necessary, and I needed him to hear me. I arrived in the lobby a few minutes before six. Paul was sitting in one of the chairs in the lounge area. Quickly, standing up, he walked over toward me. I was more nervous than ever. The last time we spoke, he was arrogant and rude at the restaurant. I had hoped that whatever he had been going through, he would've straightened it out. I didn't want a repeat of that guy. That's not the man I fell in love with. And yes, I still loved him.

His body language showed me that he was ashamed of our past encounter. He acted like we were strangers. They say time heals all wounds. I was counting on it tonight. "Mary, it's so good to see you. How have you been?" He asked with complete sincerity.

"I've been well, Paul. Thank you," I replied, trying to hide the pain from my broken heart.

"I know you said you wanted to talk, and I would love that, but before we do, would it be too presumptuous to think maybe I could still take you to the Riviera in New Jersey tonight? We still have time to get there," he asked with that sweet tone I knew and loved.

I wasn't sure how anything would play out by the night's end. Would we get past all the pain? Would Paul confide in me on what had made him so angry toward me that night? Would he tell me what he was keeping from me? There was a lot of would he's, but either way, I needed answers. Focusing on why I needed to talk to him was my main objective, but if this would be my last night ever with him, I wanted to be better than the last time.

"Sure. I would like that very much, but when we get back, we must talk. This can not wait any longer, " I stated, ensuring he understood. He agreed.

The cab ride to the nightclub took just over an hour. Neither one of us talked much. I did ask him how things were going with his job. That's when he informed me that he was considering leaving the hotel business and finding a new career path. I encouraged him in whatever endeavor he thought would make him happy. I did feel that there was something about Paul that seemed different, but I couldn't quite put my finger on it.

Silence filled the last fifteen minutes of the ride except when Paul, out of the blue, asked, "So, has your boss changed your title yet? I've been reading what you've been writing, Mary. You have a craft like no other. I can see it now: someday, you'll be sitting in that big fancy chair with your big fancy view, making all the decisions."

Although it was nice for Paul to say all that, he didn't understand. He didn't know the decisions and the sacrifices I would have to make in the next couple of days. Nothing in my life was what it once was, but I didn't want to think about any of that. I just wanted to enjoy myself for as long as I could. Answering Paul, I replied, "Maybe someday."

As the cab pulled up, the pulsating music from the club filled the air, igniting my anticipation. I was ready to leave all my worries behind and dive into a fun night. The club was perched atop the Palisades, with a man at the door diligently checking ID's. This place had a reputation for underage kids trying to sneak in, and I had heard that the owner had been fined several times, but who knows? That could be just rumors.

"Next," the man called out in a firm tone.

Paul and I handed him our IDs. He looked both of us up and down, then looked back at our IDs before waving us into the club, saying, "Enjoy your evening."

The place was breathtaking. The panoramic windows of the nightclub offered a stunning view of the twinkling lights of New York City. We secured a table near the stage just in time for the announcement that Frank Sinatra was about to perform. The anticipation was intense, and I could barely contain it. A charming, elegantly dressed waitress approached us to take our drink order.

Surprisingly, Paul ordered a club soda, and I had just a glass of Schweppes with no ice. As I waited patiently for "Ol' Blue Eyes" to grace the stage, I took in the surroundings like the rest of the crowd. When I turned, glancing over my shoulder, I spotted the legendary Bud Abbott and Lou Costello conversing with another gentleman.

My eyes widen with disbelief. I couldn't help but nudge Paul, trying to be discreet, as I pointed, "Look over your shoulder."

He chuckled and said, "Mary, they're just regular folks. It's no big deal," his calm reaction made me smile.

He didn't understand that I rarely saw a celebrity up close. I found it exciting, but he made it seem like running into famous people was his daily routine. Either way, I was in awe. Suddenly, the lights dimmed, and the crowd went wild, including myself. There he was, standing just ten feet away from me on stage. Oh, how handsome he was. The radio announced a week ago that Frank would sing a few new songs that no one had heard.

He approached the mic and asked the crowd, "Are you ready, New Jersey, to have a good time tonight?" The response was thunderous, especially from the women. I couldn't help but chuckle as one woman shouted, "I want to have your baby," and another, "Marry me, Frank." The crowd's energy was infectious.

The band started to play a few cords, and then he began to sing. His voice was pitch-perfect, and every woman gushed over him. Frank commanded the stage, and he knew it. He made sure when he sang to serenade women with his blue eyes. He even had me in his trance as he smiled past me.

Frank sang new songs, including **My Funny Valentine** and **Foggy Day** and his classics, **All of Me, As Time Goes By,** and **Young at Heart**. It didn't matter what he sang; each resonated with me. As Frank began to sing his last song for the night, **Don't Forget Tonight, Tomorrow**, Paul scooted his chair closer to me. Smiling, he said, "I've missed you, Mary."

My feelings for Paul were a tangled mess, a conflict I couldn't untangle. I missed him, but I knew everything was about to change. I didn't want to ruin the little time we had left listening to Frank, so I said, "Me too."

The evening ended with Frank singing to over a thousand people. Paul and I will never forget that we were two of those people that night. When we arrived back at the hotel, it was well past eleven, and although I was tired, I couldn't put off the conversation I needed to have with Paul. I invited him back to my room, and he obliged. I didn't have an extra chair like Paul in his room, so we both had to sit on the bed facing one another.

As I sat there, vulnerable and uncertain, I knew I had to start the conversation. I took a deep breath and began, "Paul, when I first came to New York, I had set my sights on a career here. It took courage to leave my only home and live the life I always dreamed of in a city where I knew no one. It was scary, yet exciting. Every day was a new adventure, and I awaited my big break. My plans didn't include having a romantic relationship or falling in love, but you came along, and I fell in love anyway. I'm not sure…"

"Mary, I don't mean to cut you off, but if I don't speak now, I may never find the courage to be honest with you, and you deserve my honesty."

Right then and there, I felt that whatever he was about to tell me would forever change our lives. Yet, I knew what I would say to him would forever change our lives. The look on his face wasn't the look I was used to. Besides that unfortunate incident a month ago, things were always good between us, but now the moment has come.

He reached for my hand and said, " Let me start by telling you how truly sorry I am. Sorry thatI wasn't honest with you from the beginning. There are things in my past I'm not proud of and choices I've made that I'm trying to undo, but it's not easy. I need you to know that from the moment we met, you gave me the purpose to be better and to do better, yet I have failed you. You were the last person I ever wanted to upset or scare, and I know I did just that on the last night we were together at the restaurant. If I could take it all back, I would, but I know I can't. Everything was going good until she called."

Silence filled the air. No traffic noise came from the streets outside my window, and the annoying drip from the bathroom faucet dissipated. Even the soft ticking on my watch seemed to stop. Time stood still, yet the only thing that continued was the tears that slowly trickled down my face. It was hard to breathe. It felt like someone was crushing my windpipe, stopping me from taking in air. His words, "**she called**," were like a record skipping, repeatedly taunting me.

I pulled my hand from his and told him not to touch me. I couldn't believe what he said. Why? Why would he do this to me? Did he have a family somewhere else? I took a deep breath, wiped the tears from my face, and asked as calmly as possible, "Who's she, Paul?"

"Getting off the bed, he paced back and forth a few times before saying, "Please, you have to know I love you, not her."

Quickly stopping him from continuing, I asked, "Your wife, I presume?"

"Yes, but I left her a long time ago. I didn't love her anymore. I've been fighting to divorce her, but she won't sign the papers. That's who I was on the phone with. She's the one who pushed my buttons. She's the one…."

I interjected his mere rambling. I couldn't take it anymore. I had to do what was best for me and our baby. Before asking him to leave my room, I said, " What you did was wrong. You took away my choice. You didn't give me a chance to decide for myself. Whether you were too afraid of my answer or didn't care, you were wrong, Paul. I can't do this, and I won't. Someone once said that a man will treat you precisely how he thinks of you, and how I see it, you weren't thinking of me—only yourself. I'm sorry, but I want you to leave."

That night, I watched as he walked out the door. I knew it broke him as it broke me. I needed and wanted him, yet I was not important enough for him to be honest with me. From then on, I had to figure out what I would do for myself and my baby. I wouldn't do what Paul did and take away his decision to be in our child's life. No, I would give him the opportunity, but on my terms. The only thing I could do for myself was be a good mom, and that's what I planned on doing.

Early the following day, I called my mother to tell her everything. Knowing her unconditional love and care for me, I wasn't afraid of her response. She has always been my rock, supporting every decision I've made, even when she had reservations. As much as I cherished my job and life in New York, the time had come to return home. I found solace in my mother's unwavering support, knowing she would be there to help me raise my child.

Before I planned to leave, I found it challenging to face Paul for the next couple of days. The pain was too raw, and I knew I'd be tempted to stay because, despite everything, I still loved him. But the trust between us was shattered, and the fact that he was married didn't sit well with me, even if he wanted to divorce her. As I sorted out my affairs, Paul was persistent, writing letters and slipping them under my hotel door. I couldn't bring myself to read them; I just stored them in one of my shoeboxes and left them there. I admit, I did stare at them, but that's as far as I could go.

On Friday, I went to work and informed Dan about my decision to return home. The news saddened him, but he was understanding and supportive, wishing me the best. I didn't delve into the specifics, and he didn't pry. I penned a letter to James, expressing my gratitude for the opportunity and his belief in me, and asked Dean to deliver it the next time they met. He agreed.

Before bidding New York farewell, I had one more critical stop: Saint Patrick's Cathedral. I couldn't leave without meeting Sister Mary one last time. Her influence on my life was profound, and I felt she needed to understand the depth of her impact on me. I stepped into the church, overwhelmed by a flood of emotions. I found solace in the familiar pews, the cathedral's grandeur, and God's presence. Watching others light candles and offer prayers, I couldn't help but feel a deep sense of loss. Tears welled up in my eyes, and I wept, wondering if this was how Jesus felt when his heart broke for the world. The pain was unbearable, and I questioned if I would ever find love again.

As I wiped away my tears, I heard a familiar voice, "Mary, darling, what's wrong?"

I turned around to see Sister Mary standing there, bathed in the soft light of the stained glass window. She looked like an angel sent from heaven. I was momentarily speechless, then stood and replied, "Everything, Sister."

As we returned to her office, Sister Mary reached for my hand. Despite the seemingly mundane surroundings of four walls, I found a profound sense of safety in her touch. Knowing Sister Mary's love for me mirrored her love for the Lord was comforting. "Please, Mary, take a seat," she offered, pointing to the leather chair across from her desk.

Seated, I accepted Sister Mary's tissue. As I wiped away the tears, I couldn't help but feel the weight of my vulnerability. I noticed Sister Mary's Bible on her desk, which caused me to ask her, "Is there anything in there that states how long it takes someone to heal from a broken heart?"

"Oh my dear, if it were that easy. So, he's broken your heart. I'm so sorry. Do you want to talk about it?" she asked.

The words spilled out before I could stop myself, "He's married, and I'm pregnant." The weight of my confession hung heavy in the air.

"I can see now why you are crying. It's more than just a break-up. I want to be honest with you but also gentle and respectful. What I'm about to tell you isn't to add to your pain but to guide you toward healing. I've always been honest with you, right?" she asked.

I nodded in agreement and replied, "Yes, Sister."

"When we find ourselves in a situation where we want the pain to go away, we ask God to remove the pain. The God I serve loves you and allows suffering so that we may draw closer to Him. Some may see this as a cruel God, but I see it as one who gives us the freedom to choose.

Sometimes, we may feel alone, but we are never truly alone. God is always there, waiting for us to turn to Him for help. Worrying about your future won't bring you peace, but allowing God to guide you will lead you in the right direction. Remember this advice as you heal from betrayal and a broken heart. You always want to be someone's choice, not their option. You deserve someone who sees the value you bring into their life and your relationship.

It's okay to let your soul cry tears. It cleanses your heart and helps it heal. At the end of all your heartache, your heart will lead you to where you belong. That's all the advice I have besides prayer, Mary. I'm a little rusty about the love from a man, not from God, though," Sister Mary reveals with sincerity and a kind smile.

"Thank you for your kindness, advice, and love. I have a tough road ahead, but I know I'll get through it. I've chosen to return home, where I'll get help and support from my mother and family. I'm scared but determined to do the right thing for my child, " I expressed.

"Does this gentleman know he's going to be a father?" Sister Mary asked.

"Not as this time he doesn't, but I will tell him. I'm still processing this myself. I would never keep this from him, even though he kept his wife a secret. My child deserves a father. Whether he chooses to be part of my child's life will be up to him," I expressed.

"Well, that's very mature of you, Mary. I'm writing down my number and the church's address. If you ever need to talk, please call me. And the address is so you can send me a picture of your precious little boy."

I smiled and said, "Boy, I don't even know what my baby will be."

Sister Mary confessed, "I have my connections."

We both chuckled, which was nice. She knew I needed something to distract me from my heartache. Before I hugged her goodbye, she handed me a tiny envelope with a piece of paper inside. She told me not to open it for at least ten years. Her request was a little strange, to say the least. I asked her why, and she responded, "In ten years, you will know, and then you will decide." The weight of her words made me wonder what my future held.

It sounded foolish, but I wouldn't question someone who served the Lord. After leaving the church, I headed back to the hotel, where I informed Sergio that I was checking out of the hotel in the morning. He said, "I will be sad to see you leave, Mary. You have been a pleasant guest and a wonderful friend to talk to. I'll miss you." Of course, I asked him to do me one more favor before I left, not to mention it to Paul.

I headed toward my room to pack up my stuff before relaxing. I was glad I didn't buy much stuff while I was here, seeing everything fit in my suitcases. When I was done, I showered before sitting on the bed to eat the sandwhich I grabbed from the corner vendor. Nothing was entertaining on the TV, so I grabbed the Agatha Christie book I bought and began to read it, hoping I would get tired.

I awoke the following day with the book on the floor and my reading glasses still on my face. The burden of the previous day's events still hung heavily on me, and I felt a profound sense of brokenness. All I wanted to do was stay in bed and cry, but I needed to get ready. My bus ticket time was noon. I'd arrived back home sometime after six. I was engulfed in a whirlwind of emotions. Part of me longed to talk to Paul, but the other part just wanted to get home and figure out where I would go from all this.

Pulling back the curtains, I looked out the window, contemplating my life's path. The uncertainties rushed in like a crashing wave. I yearned to rewind time, but the truth was, I couldn't. I could, however, move forward, and that's what I intended to do. In his kindness, Sergio arranged for a different bellhop to assist me with my bags and take me to the waiting cab. He reassured me that Paul was out running an errand, so I didn't have to worry. With an unwavering spirit, I stepped forward, feeling the weight of the past lift off my shoulders.

As the bellhop assisted the cab driver with loading my suitcases, I stopped to thank Sergio for his kindness and generosity during my six-month stay at the hotel. He said it was a pleasure to have me as a guest and that I should stop by if I ever found myself back in New York.

I told myself not to look back as the cab drove away, and I didn't. It took roughly six and a half hours to return home; each passing mile was a step closer to my mother's arms. The entire time on the bus, I stayed by myself. I read my book, which allowed me to escape from the world for a while. As the cab driver helped me get my suitcases to my front porch, I noticed my mother peering out the front window. The door swung open, and immediately she cried out as she wrapped her arms around me tight, "Oh, Mary. My sweet Mary."

Her embrace broke me. I cried in her arms like a child. Every part of me needed her to heal my brokenness. After a few minutes, I had to remind her that we were standing on the porch and the neighbors were probably watching as most of them were nosey. She said, "Let them. I don't care. You are my child." Her reaction to my return was overwhelming, making me realize how much I was missed.

We sat at the kitchen table for a few hours, drinking hot tea and eating freshly baked pie while we cried together, and even though there were still so many uncertainties, I was home. I got back on the horse once I overcame my pity party. I needed to stay focused on my child, so I went back to the job I originally left. The company I had previously worked for took me back without hesitation as they valued my work. I even got a small bump in my pay.

Over the next year, I received ten letters from Paul. Sergio called to ask if he could give Paul my address so he could write to me. I allowed it because I was in a good place and had control over my future. I told him about the baby, our son Russell, and although he wasn't in a position to do as much as he would've liked, he did send me money when he could. We stayed in touch as much as possible.

Paul informed me how he had been sick, and the doctors in New York had a hard time treating him as they were unsure what was causing his illness. I allowed him to call and talk, making it more accessible, as sometimes he didn't feel good enough to write. As far as I knew, he was still married, never mentioning that he was divorced, yet I never bothered to ask. Throughout time, I had come to accept the path my life had taken, and though I could never be with Paul, I did continue to love him as we shared a child. For that, I would be forever grateful.

I received a letter on December 3, 1954, read,

"Dear Mary, I'm enclosing twenty dollars, hoping this will help for the time being. I had to borrow part of it, but with Christmas coming, I may be able to take care of the rest by then. The doctor told me that I would need to rest as I was losing too much weight. I am down to one hundred thirty-seven pounds and can't hold any food down. Maybe I'll improve, but I'll have to abide by his advice if I don't. I'll try to write again soon.

Sincerely, P.

I couldn't help but think, what if something happened to Paul, and my son never had the chance to meet his father? The thought tormented me, but I used what I thought was my better judgment and waited until he asked about his father. At age five, that day came when I was asked, "Where is my dad? Why do all my friends have one, but I don't?" It wasn't easy to explain, but I did my best. I did try to stay in contact with Paul for as long as possible, but the letters stopped coming.

In the summer of 1960, I took my Russell, who was now six, back to New York, hoping he would finally meet his dad and maybe have a relationship with him. My search for Paul stopped when I discovered that the hotel where he was working was sold, and he left. I tried finding him through the doctor he once told me about, but I had no luck. He didn't even know what happened to Paul. I was heartbroken for my child. All I could do was head back home and continue to be a good mother while trying to satisfy my child's need for his dad with stories. If I'm being honest, I was never the same that day.

Chapter Fourteen

Many years have passed, and I've tried giving Russell the best life possible. I've solely focused on the gift Paul blessed me with rather than the loss I felt that day years ago. I've just celebrated my fiftieth birthday. One of the gifts I received from my sister Bea was a new purse; as she continuously pointed out, I've had the same one for over twelve years. This old purse, a constant companion in my frugal life, held more than just my belongings. It carried the weight of memories, both joyful and painful.

While taking all my stuff out of my old purse and transferring it to the new one, I came across the small envelope Sister Mary gave me years ago. The tear in the side of the purse caused it to slip between the lining all the years. Stuck to it was Paul's fortune cookie paper I took that night at the restaurant. The unexpectedness of finding it after all these years was overwhelming. I couldn't believe it.

I first carefully removed Paul's fortune, trying not to tear it. Each fold and each crease held a piece of the past, and I handled it with the utmost care. Then, I placed the envelope on the table where I was sitting. Unfolding the fortune in bold letters, it read, "**A Part Of Us Remain Wherever We Have Been**." I felt a wave of emotions crashing over me, and without any control, I wept. I sat thinking of all the moments I had shared with Paul. The tears I cried were not of sadness anymore. They were of gratitude for the love I got to experience with him and my child. Placing the fortune aside, I opened the envelope I had received from Sister Mary. Before pulling the small note out, I reflected on my first encounter with her and smiled. She helped me out of the darkness and into the light, and I have been forever grateful.

I unfolded the note. It contained a quote from Maya Angelou: "**There is no greater agony than bearing an untold story inside you.**" Those words profoundly resonated with me. Thinking about it now, I've realized that no matter how much things have hurt along the way, I've been able to look back and know they have changed my life for the better.

The time I spent in New York in nineteen fifty-three will always hold a special place in my heart. The lessons I learned and the people I met have been with me even now. Isabella and I have stayed friends over the years. She's even come up to Massachusetts with Mateo several times for a visit. Isabella's faith in God still stands strong today. She and Mateo take time to serve at food banks, collect clothes for the less fortunate, and pray over many while spreading love, hope, and the gospel of Jesus.

As for Sister Mary, even though we stayed in touch as much as possible, she passed away five years ago from an inoperable brain tumor. I visited her just a few months before her passing. I will say my heart broke. I remember I asked her, "Are you scared?"

Her response was so confident, "You know, I think I would be if I didn't know and love Jesus. I've spent my entire life serving Him, and now I get to be with him. When I gave my life to the Lord over fifty-five years ago, I found peace, and now I will continue that peace in heaven. Can I share something with you before you go?" she asked, even though she always knew my answer.

"Yes, of course, "I replied.

"Remember, all you need is encouragement and belief in yourself. You will face many challenges, but know that God is molding you for greatness. Never forget it is a process. Without pain, you wouldn't grow. Whatever pain you endure, embrace it. When you walk with God, you'll sacrifice many things in this world, but He will provide what you need. I have known you for many years now, Mary, and you have gone through many obstacles, yet you have overcome them. Continue pushing forward and never give up. You are never alone."

That was the last time I spoke with Sister Mary. Shortly after, I received a phone call telling me she had passed away. I did take the time to attend her beautiful service. Many people spoke that day on behalf of the person she was. The church couldn't hold the number of attendees, and people were standing outside the church to pay their respects. I was forever grateful to her.

Over the years, I've sat and thought about how my life became what it is today, and I wouldn't change it for anything. Yes, I took a chance on love, and it didn't work how I had hoped, but on April 8, 1954, I became a mom to a wonderful, healthy baby boy. The day we both locked eyes on each other was when I knew he would be my everything. Believe it or not, he took away all my worries. He gave me all the purpose I needed to become something I never imagined: a mother.

I was fortunate enough to have my mother by my side, guiding me through the ups and downs of motherhood. Her wisdom and patience were invaluable, and I often leaned on her for advice. She was there to help me correct my mistakes and become the best I could be for my son. It would be a lie to say I didn't think about Paul often. It was hard not to, as I raised our son into a man. I had always hoped to get another letter or a phone call, but it's been too long. I had to realize that I probably would never hear from him again after I found out he was no longer in New York. There were too many 'maybe's' for me to chase.

As for my love life, Paul was it. I never bothered much after him. I did go on a few casual dates, but none of the men were what I thought my son and I deserved. Russell has always wanted me to find love again, but he's been the only love I've ever needed.

As my story ends, I need you to know, Russell, that although you've never known your father, you are just as much a part of him as you are me. I've thought back to all the specifics I could share with you of who he was, so I made a list.

1. He was tall. At least over six feet. That's where you get your height.

2. He had hazel eyes that could peer into your soul.

3. He was a sharp dresser. He always wore a suit when he wasn't in his work uniform.

4. He always had me laughing at his corny jokes. He said it was so he could enjoy my beautiful smile. You get your corniness from him.

5. He was very generous with whatever he had.

6. He always ensured he walked on the side where the curb was. He said you can never trust a cab driver in New York City.

7. He had good taste in music. That's where you get your love for collecting 8- tracks, forty-fives, and albums.

8. He talked about how much he loved his mother. You have that in common. (Thank you)

9. I know he loved you. There has never been a doubt in my mind. You've loved all three of your children unconditionally, this I know.

10. He loved me. I know he felt I was the right person for him, and maybe that was true in a different lifetime.

I have loved you from the moment you took your first breath and when you took your first step. I have watched you become a wonderful, kind-hearted person who loves without limits. You are a great father and friend. I couldn't be more proud of who you become.

My son, may you know that everything I did was to get to this point in your life—to tell my story so that you can have some peace when I'm no longer here. Before I end this, I want you to know why I've titled this book "**The Untold Story of My Love**." The Bible reads in **Jeremiah 1:15,** *" I chose you before I formed you in the womb; I set you apart before you were born. I appointed you a prophet to the nations."*

Although that passage is God speaking, I felt God spoke to me the day I found out I was pregnant with you, saying, " **This child will be your story**." So, Russell, my untold story isn't the love I once had for your father; it's the love I've always had for you. **You Are My Story.**

Chapter Fifteen

Russell- Same day

1996

I close the book, lean against the wall, and take a few moments to absorb everything I've just read. The memories I've shared with my mother have always been a mix of joy and sorrow. The fact that she took the time to write this and leave it for me is a testament to her love and understanding. She knew about the void I felt for my father, and it was never a reflection on her. She was correct; as a child and even now, I've always felt a part of me missing. But I am forever grateful for the precious gift she has left me.

Present- 2024

2004, I was consumed by wanting to know more about my father. I yearned for details that even my mother was unaware of. Did I have any siblings, or was I an only child? Were there any hereditary diseases I should be concerned about? When and where did he die? These questions haunted me. With the unwavering support of my friends Mark and Joyce, we embarked on a journey to uncover the answers I had been searching for.

As an only child, the revelation was bittersweet. I couldn't help but wonder what I might have learned if I had a sibling whom our father had raised. However, my disappointment was assuaged when I discovered cousins scattered across different states through Ancestry.com. After reaching out, I had a heartfelt conversation with one of them. Her stories and memories of my father bridged the gap, connecting me to him in a way I had never imagined.

Not too long ago, I received several pictures of him, which are included in the book, and a family member gifted me a few pieces of his jewelry that were left to them. Paul Rouleau was born in Montana in 1898. My mother and my father were eighteen years apart. He died at the age of seventy-two and was buried in Washington. I was just sixteen. His brother Harry signed his death certificate, and within four years, Harry was laid to rest next to him.

Over the years, I've pieced together as much information as possible on my dad and his family. Sometimes, I wished I had asked my mother more questions. Maybe there were things she had forgotten to tell me. Either way, I have to find peace with what I do know. With the love I have for my mother, although she has passed away, I can say she did a fantastic job loving me and teaching me, and now I understand her story.